STATE OF
VENGEANCE

By

JOHN NOONAN

To my wife Catherine for her patience,

To Mark for his advice.

CONTENTS

CHAPTER 1

There was an almighty crack of noise followed by a few seconds of total silence as Jack was making his way towards the door of the pub, the whole place shook violently with the vibration of a massive explosion. The glass windows shattered in on top of the elderly couple who sat in the same seats that he had seen them in earlier, they were probably the same seats in the pub that they sat on for their couple of glasses of Guinness every morning for years. Jack instinctively knew it was a bomb, the noise was followed by a deadly quietness, he counted out a couple of seconds before he ran out through the broken door which was lying off its hinges, the sound of screaming people and glass falling all around greeted him. There were people lying all over the place, some with arms and legs missing and blood was everywhere. The moment he left the pub, the ceiling collapsed on top of the barman, covering him in plaster. Jack never gave him a thought.

He could hear screaming from the elderly woman in the pub, along with the people lying on the ground, in the distance in front of him. Looking up the street along the LUAS tracks, a couple of hundred yards away, he could not believe his eyes – the tram was split in half with billowing smoke and massive flames everywhere.

"Oh, Jesus Christ! Anne and Ciaran are on that," he screamed out loud.

He ran towards the train, but after a couple of strides he had to stop because his lungs were on fire. He violently threw up all that was inside him against a wall and he took several breaths but still could not move. "Fuck, fuck, fuck," he cursed, inwardly.

The sound of sirens from fire brigades, Garda cars and alarms from buildings were all that could be heard above the screams of the people. Before he could move, the street was cordoned off. Jack searched in his pockets for his mobile phone and tried to ring his ex-partner. The sweat was rolling down his face and the automatic voice on the phone told him that he had not enough credit to make the call.

"Fuck it! Fuck it!" he screamed, looking wildly around him.

He made his way over to a Garda who had run to the scene from the courthouse which was his normal place of duty and was attempting to cordon off the street.

"I have to get to that LUAS," Jack shouted, "… my son is on it."

"Get the fuck away from here now!" the Garda shouted, himself in a state of shock.

But Jack persisted in his effort to get to the scene of the carnage.

"I've told you to fuck off away from here now and don't be causing any disturbance. There are a lot of people up there doing their best to help those who are hurt and trying to get some order in place without the likes of you, full of drink, getting in their way," the harassed Garda shouted at Jack.

"Don't you hear me? You bollix! My son and his mother are on that LUAS!" Jack screamed.

The Garda took a long, pitiful look at Jack.

"I could arrest you right this minute for your abusive language, but if your son was on that LUAS they will all be taken to James Hospital, so that's the place for you," he said.

Jack stared hard at the Garda.

"Thanks," he muttered, as he turned and made his way, on foot, to the hospital, his mind was in turmoil as he went over the events of the day so far…

Jack groaned loudly as he woke up from yet another drunken slumber on the sofa in his one bedroom flat. He hadn't changed out of his filthy clothes in weeks and they smelt of sweat and piss. *"I feel like shit,"* he thought, as he glanced at the old alarm clock on the mantelpiece: it said nine o'clock. He visualised the clock's face taunting him, saying: "Yeah! You fool. You've fucked up again."

He sat up and with shaking hands lit a cigarette. He inhaled deeply and started to splutter and cough up what seemed like part of his lungs. After the violent coughing subsided, he bent forward on the sofa and squashed the butt out on the floor alongside hundreds of other cigarette burns on the filthy lino.

Jack shuffled over to the window and pulled back the filthy net curtains that had once been snow white, but now were in shreds. They barely covered the dirt-encrusted windows. He stood there for a while and watched the people walking and driving to work, the people who were making up the sane world outside.

He had to move himself, he knew that he had to be in court for 11 o'clock to fight for access to his young son, the only good thing that was left in his life. Jack made his way to the bathroom of his small Corporation flat. It had only just been given to him after months of pressure by an old friend, who was a long-serving Councillor on the Dublin Corporation. Without that help, Jack knew in his heart he'd be out on the streets now.

"Jesus, I'm in a heap," he whispered to himself, his heart heavy at the mess he was now.

He turned on the cold water tap, but nothing came out... not even a drop.

"Ah, bollix!" Jack shouted. "No fuckin' water again!"

Yet another unpaid bill he muttered – and not for the first time, he knew.

Jack left the flat and called into the cyber café and baggage holding centre on the corner of the street to use the bathroom.

"Morning Jack," said the Arab proprietor, Mustapha, with a hint of disdain in his voice, but Jack was still too hungover to recognise it.

Mustapha had come to Ireland over ten years ago after securing refugee status. He arrived with the ambition of studying medicine, but that was just a broken dream now. Prior to coming to Ireland, Mustapha had spent several weeks living in a refugee camp in the Lebanon after his Palestinian parents had been brutally murdered by the Israeli armed forces during an invasion of their homeland back in the 70s. Mustapha's uncle and the remaining elders of his family had financed his passage and seen him through university in Ireland, but before he could finish his education, the money stopped coming and he was then forced to drop out.

Internet Cafes were just beginning to open up around Dublin and a Muslim friend of his offered to get him started in one. Mustapha did not know just how many strings were attached to this apparent act of kindness, but over the years since then he had been called on to repay it in many ways, most of which were not legal.

"Morning Mus. Just need to use the gents," Jack said, pointing to the door at the back where the bathroom was, in the middle of a bank of lockers.

Jack noticed that most of the computer bays were occupied with young Arab men. He glanced curiously at some of the computer screens, assuming that they were playing video games because of the way they spoke in excited voices. Jack was fluent in Arabic although he had not used it, or heard it used, for a long time – a language that he had learned years before in the many training camps that he had attended in Libya in another life, as an active member of the IRA.

Jack suddenly stopped in his tracks when he caught some of what they were talking about. He shook his head and thought, *'No, I must be hearing things.'* He stopped at the bathroom door for a moment, unsure of what exactly he had just heard – words that sounded to him like Sacrifice! Allah! Heaven!

His mind started to reflect back on his time in the Middle East. The Arabic words swirled around in his head, echoing in a chorus of voices of excited young men. His mind searched for the meaning. Sacrifice… Allah… heaven… sacrifice… Allah… heaven… then there was the heat. The heat was the unbearable memory he associated with the Arabic part of the world. The noisy business being conducted in Martyrs Square. That was what he remembered. Farmers, butchers, spice vendors, silk merchants. The crowded trade centre of Tripoli, a hundred times bigger than Moore Street was how he tried to describe it to those who had never experienced it. And the heat. Jesus! It was unbearable. How could people live and work in that heat? It was too hot to sleep at night for fuck's sake!

The eerie sound of the lone voice from the mosque calling the faithful to prayer. The dust always in the air. The smell of food being cooked. Camels braying as they rested, from their long journeys, in the Square. The magical, wonderful and frightening sights, sounds and smells that overwhelmed an inner city Dub who had never travelled out of Ireland before the trip to Libya.

"This is what we have for you, Jock."

Three weeks here and Colonel Said Ahmad still couldn't get his name right. He was one to talk. He couldn't understand most of what was being said to him even when they spoke English!

He put his hand on Jack's shoulder and guided him across the drill courtyard and in the direction of the armory at the rear of Bab al-Aziza, the largest Libyan Revolutionary Army barracks in Tripoli. As they walked, Jack thought it looked like a palace from an Ali Baba film he often watched as a kid. It was out of place in the barracks with its artillery battery units, tanks and military vehicles.

Col. Ahmad smiled as he caught Jack transfixed on the building.

"That is a residence for the Brotherly Leader of the Revolution."

"Who?" Jack asked, feeling a little awkward as the words left his mouth.

"The Colonel. Al-Gaddafi."

"Gaddafi!" Jack exclaimed silently. "Fuckin' hell!"

He stared towards the armory again and continued a business like stride to try to conceal his inner excitement at the closest he had come to the famous Libyan leader.

The last time he was that excited was when he had got the nod to travel to Libya on behalf of the Irish Republican Army when Colonel Gaddafi, through a number of emissaries and go-betweens, had established secret contact with the Army Council in Dublin to again offer arms and finance. He had provided similar support in the early 1970s, which came to an end when a ship laden with five tonnes of weaponry was intercepted and seized by the Irish

Government. His antagonism with Britain was revived when the warlike Margaret Thatcher came to power and he reached out again to the IRA in the wake of the Hunger Strikes of 1981, which gave enormous worldwide sympathy to the cause of Irish freedom.

The Army Council deliberated carefully on who should travel. High profile personnel were ruled out due to the risk of being identified. Jack was held in high regard due to his imprisonment in the infamous Maze prison in the early 1970s. There were few Dublin volunteers actively fighting at that time in the occupied six counties after hostilities exploded in the North of Ireland in 1969. He was told later that the reason he was sent was that he could be trusted and depended upon, but most of all he would have a good chance of travelling to Libya without being detected. Jack had thought it had been decided by the toss of a coin, or no one else wanted to go.

Col. Ahmad rapped on the giant door to the armoury. A slot swung back and a guard immediately opened what seemed like four bolts that held the door secure. The guard stiffened in salute to Ahmad as he passed without acknowledging the guards' presence. Another officer appeared as they approached the opening to a brightly lit courtyard. He kissed Col. Ahmad on both cheeks and greeted him warmly. He turned to Jack and cleared his throat and began his rehearsed welcome.

"I am honoured with the meet of the Republican Army of the Ireland."

Col. Ahmad kept back a smile as he nodded approval of Sergeant al-Magrahbi's first attempt at the English language.

Slightly fazed, Jack offered his hand out to shake and said the only thing he could think of at that time and uttered in Irish, "Go raibh mile maith agat."

Col. Ahmad and al-Magrahbi looked at each blankly not sure what Jack had said.

Ahmad broke the awkward silence by inviting the sergeant to proceed, who then turned about heel and gestured Jack and Col. Ahmad to follow.

In the centre of the courtyard was a large stone daize. Resting on it was a large rectangular wooden box. Al-Magrahbi opened two steel clips and lifted the lid up.

Jack was stunned by the contents as its shape was revealed. Col. Ahmad waited until Jack had composed himself before continuing.

"The People's Revolutionary Army of Libya offers a token of support to our brothers in the Republican Army of Ireland to defeat the English imperialists," al-Magrabhi said, as he took the weapon from the box and began to assemble its accessories. "This is a Soviet made S-7 Dvina."

"I know," Jack interrupted, "a surface-to-air missile. We've heard all about them but I've never seen one." His mind raced with the possibilities of uses his comrades could put this machine to.

"This weapon will avenge your martyrs," Ahmed continued, "and strike fear into the heart of Thatcher."

Jack was thinking that thought exactly.

Al-Magrahbi held the weapon over his shoulder to demonstrate how it should be used. His voice rose as he continued his passionate instruction. Jack stared at him intently, despite being oblivious to understanding a single word he was listening to. Al-Magrabhi concluded his speech with spittle coming from his mouth and tears in his eyes. Jack could make only the last word, he roared 'Allah' as his punched his own fist to his heart.

Ahmed waited for al-Magrahbi to finish. Thanked him then dismissed him.

"He wanted to explain to you that this weapon is more than a piece of machinery. It is a symbol of how God helps his people. We are both fighting great enemies. They have greater armies, greater weapons and great stores of gold. These weapons help us fight our enemies. In our language, these weapons are called the vengeance of God."

*

Jack snapped back to the mirror in the internet cafe toilet. He felt slightly dazed as if he had just woken from a dream.

"No!" he said to himself. "It must be this head of mine still in a heap from the booze." He walked on into the bathroom and turned on the cold water tap and threw some over his head. He took a broken comb out of his jacket pocket and he tried to put his hair into some sort of shape. With his bloodshot eyes, he looked at himself in the mirror again and sighed at the reflection of a real mess gazing back at him. He could not quite take in the face that looked back at him; gone was a full head of curly blond hair, now it was scraggily, unkempt and dirty brown with plenty of grey flecks throughout; and where his face had once been considered handsome by many women, now it was ghost white in colour with plenty of wrinkled lines, puffed out areas and red blotches from the booze.

He took a step back from the mirror and looked his body up and down. Jack had always kept himself in a trim and good shape but now he was flabby in parts, with a slight beer belly. He was weak looking. He sucked in his protruding belly and puffed out his chest.

"I'll have to do something about the shape I'm in," he said to his reflection. But then his mind quickly turned to a craving for booze. "But first you need a drink, Jack, me boy," he continued to say.

He left the bathroom and thanked Mustapha and made his way towards the exit back out onto the bustling street. Mustapha stood behind the counter eying him with a mixture of pity and distaste. Just as he was opening the door to leave, Jack noticed that a group of the young Arabs were standing at the end of the row of steel lockers around an older man who was dressed in religious garb. Jack observed him opening several lockers and handing out rucksacks to two of the young men.

Jack stood outside and lit a cigarette; as he did so, the two young men with the rucksacks went outside to some of the other young Arabs. They began hugging and kissing each other, with the two with the rucksacks getting most of the attention.

Suddenly, a black van with tinted windows pulled up beside the Arabs and the older man in the religious garb left the café and got into the front passenger seat. He rolled down the window and waved a blessing out at the two men with the rucksacks. Again, Jack thought he heard the same alarming words that had caused him earlier to pause for a second, but he shook his head again. "Fuck that, I've enough to be getting on with," he muttered to himself and made his way on foot towards the Family Court.

When he reached Smithfield Square, a large cobblestoned area near the Courts, Jack impulsively decided to slip into a pub on the corner beside the LUAS train stop. He looked around, it was a miserable looking dive, he noticed that the only people there were an elderly couple and they were being tended to by a right miserable looking bastard who stared at him, he ordered a quick whisky. As he knocked back the drink in one mouthful, his body shuddered for a second, kick starting into life. He looked out the window and watched one of the many LUAS trams stop. He could see lots of solicitor types getting off, some struggling with bundles of files under their arms, others pulling little trollies behind them stacked with cardboard boxes, suited up and polished shoes and some with their white curly wigs on and flowing black gowns, all on the way to make big fees on people's suffering, he thought to himself.

He left the pub and walked through the automatic glass doors of the Family Court, pushing his way through the many split families who were there to try and sort out the unworkable situations that they found themselves in for many different reasons.

One woman he noticed was crying while pleading with a guy that looked to be in his 30s, who was standing there drawing on a cigarette, ignoring her cries, she had two little girls with her that looked to be around 10 and 12 years of age. Jack could see that she had made an effort to turn them out well with neatly clean clothes and their hair in pony tails held up with frayed ribbons, but the man would not hear of not going into court, he wanted his piece of paper saying that he had rights to the children, he needed that for the Social Welfare, so he could claim a few bob extra, Jack knew his sort. Another couple were arguing about money, the man was pleading that he was unemployed and that she was getting what she was due, but Jack could hear that she had stopped his visits because she believed that he was earning good money while working on the side, a friend of hers had told her. Jack noticed another woman sitting in the corner listening to a man begging her to come home, that the children were missing her, that he was missing her, that he forgave her for what she had done. The troubles of the world could be heard in that waiting area of the Family Law Court.

"This is not me," Jack said to himself, "I'm not like any of these men here."

He was just about to get up and leave when he heard his name and Anne's been called. He hadn't noticed Anne until she walked forward with a guy in a suit carrying a bunch of folders under his arm.

"I'm fucked here," he said to himself, sorry now that he never bothered to get a solicitor of his own, but then where was the money coming from for that? He feared the worst.

His prediction was correct. The judge threw the book at him and sided with his ex-wife. Afterwards, a dejected-looking Jack was standing on the steps outside the courthouse arguing with his ex-partner Anne and her solicitor, while his young son, Ciaran, was standing behind his mother crying loudly.

"You couldn't even turn up in court for your own son without the smell off drink on yah," Anne said bitterly.

"I only had the one," Jack pleaded, "for fuck sake, you have to let me see him. he's all I have."

"Just fuck off away from us… you heard what the judge said, so in future if you want to ask me anything, get your solicitor to contact my solicitor – and stay to fuck away from us," Anne said, in a firm controlled voice.

Jack moved towards her and her solicitor stepped in front of him.

"Go away now, Mr Maguire, or I'll have you arrested for harassing this woman," he said, looking around for the duty Garda.

"Fuck off you! Yeh little bollix," Jack snarled, as he walked off.

He caught his son's eye as both he and his mother boarded the LUAS. The young lad gave a little wave and a smile, which broke Jack's heart. He stood there watching and waving back as the automatic doors closed and the tram pulled away, with the now well-known *ding ding* sound of the bell ringing out.

Dejected, Jack went back to the pub to order a pint of stout, the elderly couple were still the only ones there and the miserable looking barman looked at him as if he was being disturbed from something very important: the racing page of the paper. His mind was in a spin. The bollix of a judge had refused him access to his son, deeming him to be an unfit parent after her solicitor had given the court a full rundown on him being a former IRA leader, who for 30 years had engaged the British Army on all fronts of war both in Ireland and abroad, while ignoring his family responsibilities. Since the Peace Process, Jack had no role to play in the political goings on and had not held down a steady job. Soon after leaving the IRA, things had started a promising business for Jack when he started a security business with a friend but he soon neglected it and watched it fall apart as he sat practically every day on a high stool in the nearest bar talking shite, instead of working.

At the bar, Jack looked for his pint. The barman took his time pulling it and then placed it in front of Jack. He looked at it for a couple of seconds and turned away to leave.

"You'll have to pay for this anyway, you know," the barman said.

Jack turned back around and starred at him menacingly.

"Well maybe not… but don't bother coming back in here. You're barred," the barman shouted after him.

CHAPTER 2

When he arrived at the hospital, Jack found the place in mayhem, the reception area was packed with people, all seeking information on the dead and injured. He set about looking for a friend of his from the old days who he remembered was working there as a porter; thankfully it didn't take long to find him.

"Mick," Jack called out. "Mick, thank fuck you are still working here. I need to find out where my son and my ex are. They were on that LUAS that was hit."

"Jesus! Jack, is it really you? I haven't seen you in years," Mick said as he looked Jack up and down. His memory turned immediately to the incident that resulted in him getting the bad limp that he had. During the War, he had been on an operation with Jack's unit. He had been honoured to be asked to take part in the unit as they were known as the best in the Irish Republican Army. The operation was to capture a British army officer who was reported to be on a fishing holiday in the depths of County Kerry. All had been going well on the night in question until they approached a cottage in the middle of nowhere that their informant led them to believe housed the British officer. They knew immediately that they had walked into a trap when all hell broke loose with bullets flying in all directions. He was hit in the first salvo of bullets – a couple of rounds entered his lower back and others smashed his leg; all of which disabled him immediately.

He would never forget the sight of Jack jumping over the brick wall that surrounded the cottage and - with guns blazing and running to his side – he bravely threw him over his shoulder and retraced his steps, all the time firing his weapon at the cottage.

The Unit managed to escape, but Mick had to be left at the door of the nearest hospital. He was arrested that night and after some intense questioning by the Special Branch in his hospital room where – despite the protestations of the nursing staff – he was brutalized and then charged with the attempted murder of the British officer.

But not once did he answer any questions. As he sat in pain in the court, he was found guilty of the charge before a nonjury court which had been introduced by the Government of the day, and sentenced to ten years in prison. He never received proper medical attention in the prison, which resulted in him having a permanent limp. But Mick never forgot Jack for saving his life.

Mick told Jack, "I'll see what I can do, but you should take yourself into the toilets and clear yourself up as there is sick all down the front of you. You are in a right state... don't leave from here and I'll be back shortly with some news for ya."

"Thanks pal."

Looking at himself in the toilet mirror, Jack was horrified when he saw the actual state of himself. The front of his jacket was destroyed with vomit. He took it off and went through the pockets, which had nothing in them, before dumping it in the bin. He then splashed his face with water and dried himself off with paper tissues, and then ran his fingers through his hair to put some shape in it. Again, looking in the mirror, he felt he looked a bit better now. After about ten minutes, Mick walked into the toilet.

"Come on with me, Jack," he said, "your son is in the operating theatre as we speak, and his mother is in A and E with some minor cuts and bruising. Come on and we'll get her and I'll bring you both up to the theatre."

"Thanks, Mick," Jack said and followed him to A and E. Mick, Jack recalled, had been a good active Volunteer in the Irish Republican Army and had often been involved in backing up the Unit that Jack himself had led.

When they got to the A&E, Jack immediately spotted Anne and they both looked at each other for a moment before tightly hugging for several lingering minutes. Jack wiped the tears from her eyes.

"Come on now," Jack said, "Mick here is bringing us up to the theatre. The little fellow is there now."

The operation was still going on when they arrived at the theatre. They were placed in a waiting room. Jack thanked Mick as he left and then turned on the television that was on the wall. The news was discussing the bombing. *'Fucking hell,'* Jack thought, as he listened to how a second bomb had gone off on another LUAS train at Connolly station with many casualties. The Minister for Justice came on condemning the attacks and he implied that the terrible act may have been the work of a Dissident group of Republicans, who, he added, were all well known to the Gardaí.

"They will be hunted down throughout the length and breadth of the land until they are all behind bars," the Minister told the reporter, as he outlined a whole list of measures that he was going to introduce to stop the terrorists committing such acts again.

Jack thought, *"The Minister bloody knows that nobody is listening to what these measures are, but he's happy with that, as it means that he will have no problem getting them passed. The carnage on the trains are of no consequence to him… that fucker sees them as a means to an end. The bastard."*

After an agonising wait, Jack didn't know how long, the waiting room door opened and two doctors, both Arabs, and a nurse walked in.

"How do you do? I am Doctor Kaleem and I have good news for you – your little boy is fine and after a short period of time with us, he will go home in good health," the Doctor said.

"Thank God for that," Jack and his ex-wife said in unison.

Jack looked hard at the Doctor and felt that this was a man he could trust; by looking into his eyes he saw the same intent of purpose that he had seen in the eyes of the many young Arab Palestinians recruits that he had helped train over the years. He felt that if the Doctor said that things were good for his son, then that's the way things were, with no hidden agendas or half-truths. This was a man who looked after himself, Jack thought, both inside and out; he looked around 30 years old with no excess fat, fit looking.

Doctor Kaleem turned to his junior and gave instructions in Arabic; Jack could fully understand what was been said and was happy with what he heard. He then spoke to the two doctors in Arabic, surprising everyone in the room, none more than Anne, as he told them that he was aware what was said and thanked them both for their work.

When they left, Jack turned to his wife and said, "I can stay the night if you want to go home for a rest. I can keep you informed straight away if anything changes."

After a brief hesitation, she agreed and left. Jack spent the next few hours waiting and watching all the news coverage, some of which was interviewing survivors from both LUAS explosions, including one woman lying in a hospital bed who spoke of noticing a dark-skinned, tall man with a haversack on his back.

"What caught my attention," she told the reporter, "was his fixed smile." She went on to add that she could recall him shouting out loudly something strange just before the flash of light and the bang of the explosion went off.

Another casualty had a similar story to tell, which prompted the reporter to question the Minister's view that Dissident Republican's were responsible and he pointed out the similarity with Mid-Eastern suicide bomb attacks and the LUAS attacks. Going over the events of the day in his mind, it dawned on Jack that he had witnessed the suicide bombers getting prepared in the cyber café, which made him angry with himself that he had done nothing about it.

*

He must have dozed off because he snapped awake with the gentle nudging of Doctor Kaleem.

"I am sorry," he said, "I did not mean to startle you. Your son is fine and is sleeping peacefully at the moment. I am very interested in your knowledge of the Arabic language."

"Oh, that was a long time ago, another life," Jack said dismissively. "Doc, I have a good idea of what happened today and if I am correct, I fear that yourself and your people will have a hard time ahead."

"Please explain," the Doctor asked, pulling up a seat beside him.

Jack began to tell him all that he had seen and heard that morning in the cyber café. The Doctor listened intently.

"I fear you may be right if what you have told me turns out to be true," said the Doctor. "There are madmen attached to all religions but that does not mean that all or even many Muslim are mad. In fact, it is against the teachings of the Holy Koran to do what these people do."

"I fully understand, Doc, but please take this number and get in touch with me if you have any trouble," Jack said, writing his mobile phone number down on a piece of tissue he picked up from a tissue box off the bedside locker.

After the doctor left, Jack walked down the corridor into a one-bed ward and looked at his son lying on the bed with tubes, it seemed, sticking out of everywhere. Standing there, Jack thought of all the times that his son had asked him to go and watch him playing football or take him to a hurling match in Croke Park like other boys' fathers did, or even to help him with his homework – but Jack had always been too busy drinking. Thinking about how all that activity time with his son had been wasted – practically pissed away in the pubs – the tears began to fall down his face. He curled his hands into fists.

"Please give me a second chance to do all the things I should have done with my son," he asked out loud, to nobody.

He stood there for a while in silence.

"Don't worry little man," Jack said quietly, through clenched teeth, "I swear that those people are going to pay for what they have done to you."

After he had recomposed himself, Jack thanked the medical staff once again and made his way down to the hospital reception area to the public phone. He rang Anne, who picked up almost immediately.

"Is everything okay?" she asked worriedly.

"Yeah, the little fella is sleeping well. I'm on my way home now as there are some things that I have to get done."

"Jack, you can't leave. You promised to stay there all night and morning, like!"

"He'll be okay. He's in safe hands here. I have some things to do."

She started screaming hysterically down the phone at him about his heavy drinking. At that point, he slammed the phone down. Jack left the hospital and started walking along the empty streets towards his flat. As he walked with his head down against the slight wind and his hands in his pockets, he felt the cold with no coat. Jack felt a change come over him, he straightened up and a purpose came into his stride. He walked into his flat and looked around the place.

"What a fuckin' tip head this place is," he said out loud, walking into the bedroom. He collapsed on the bed and went into a deep sleep, fully clothed.

CHAPTER 3

Jack woke up mid-afternoon with the hope that the day and night before had been a bad dream. But turning on the television for the news shattered that hope. There was constant coverage of the bombings with debate and speculation on who could have carried out the attacks and for what reason. The Minister for Justice and the Minister for Foreign Affairs were constant faces and voices on the screen, giving their views on what needed to be done. The Justice Minister was coming under much pressure for his initial blaming of dissident Republicans. The finger of blame was now being pointed firmly at Muslim fanatics, but why would they want to attack Ireland, a neutral country?

Fed up watching the news, Jack looked around the flat and decided to get stuck in to cleaning it up. Having something to do, he felt, would help him focus on what he knew had to be done. It took him several hours to clean up. The curtains were first to go as he threw them into the rubbish bag and he then scraped clean the windows. The sweat began to pour out of him, but the place began to look and smell like somewhere that someone could actually live in.

He filled several large black plastic bags with rubbish and all the time he could hear the television in the background giving up-to-date commentary on what had happened: there were now 50 people dead and hundreds injured. After a while, Jack noticed how often the two Ministers were on giving their views. "That's not the norm," Jack thought. "Why only those two and nobody else?" he wondered.

After he had dumped the rubbish bags around the back of the house, he returned to the flat and made himself a cup of tea and sat down for a few moments. He phoned Joe Murphy who was his long suffering partner in a small security company that had been built up to run most of the pub, restaurant and club doors in the tourist hotspot area of Dublin, Temple Bar. Joe had long since took over and ran the business in Jack's drunken absence.

"Joe, Jack here," he spoke to the message minder on Joe's phone, "can you ring me back as soon as you can… bad news – me young fella, along with Anne, were caught in that explosion on the LUAS. Anne's okay, but me son's still in intensive care. I am on my way back there now. Giz a call when you get a chance."

He washed, dried and ironed some clothes. While he did so, Jack found himself in a reflective mood and his mind wondered back through the years of his life. Growing up in the council flats in the north inner city of Dublin, he was the youngest of a large family with three sisters and four brothers; his father worked in the docks, like every other man in the flats; and his mother did lots of cleaning jobs whenever or where ever she could get them. His parents where both hard working people and they, as kids, wanted for little. It only seemed like last week to him, as he thought about his upbringing, and yet he knew that he had done more in his life than most people would do in two lifetimes.

The turning point in his life happened one day as he sat down with his family to tea, it was a Sunday evening and he started watching the news footage, he was not really paying any attention to it, he was concentrating on getting the last piece of cake, but the pictures on the tele were of a protest march by thousands of people in Derry. Suddenly, as gunfire sounds could be heard on the report, his mother let out a cry of anguish and got on her knees and began praying. All of them sitting at the table went quiet and watched the television, spellbound at the pictures of soldiers shooting people. They were horrified as images of men and priests carrying bodies flashed into their front room. It looked to them like it was a Hollywood film. Jack knew then that what he was watching was not right. From that day on his life changed. There was no more hanging around the streets, no more playing football in the courtyard. Instead, Jack stole any book that he could find on the history of Ireland, mostly from the Eason's bookstore in O'Connell Street. He educated himself on the political happenings of Ireland and soon made his way into the Republican Movement at 18 years of age. He very quickly rose through the ranks of operators who were actively involved in the war against the British occupation of Ireland. After 25 years of fulltime military operations, Jack instinctively sensed that things were not going well. He knew from reading all those polemic and historical books as a teenager that history was about to repeat itself and a sell-out was on the way. After all, it had happened after the Civil War in the 1920s and also after every military campaign against the English presence in Ireland, right up to the present day. He knew that following a sell-out there would inevitably be a split in the ranks when Irishmen would turn on fellow brothers in arms.

Jack wanted no part in any of that, so he fell away from his comrades and began drifting from pub to pub, falling deeper and deeper in the black hole that he now found himself in.

Jack snapped out of his thoughts and took a shower, delighted that the water was back on. He stood under the hot tap for ages, feeling the water flush away the old Jack. He felt he was stepping out of the shower as the real Jack. He put on clean trousers and a fresh polo shirt, polished his shoes and grabbed the cleanest jacket he could find and made his way to the hospital.

It was getting dark as he walked through the hospital car park when he noticed three men viciously kicking the shite out of a man on the ground.

"You murdering Muslim," one of them shouted, as he booted the man in the stomach.

"You're only an Arab bastard," another said, spitting on their victim, who was rolled up in a ball on the ground and screaming in pain.

"Here stop that, leave it out!" Jack shouted, running towards them.

The men quickly scattered. Jack bent down to help the man.

"Doctor Kaleem!" Jack said, shocked. "Are you alright?"

"I guess that you were right, Mister Maguire… the bigots are loose…" the Doctor replied. "Don't worry about me; I am fine. There will hopefully just be outward bruising on my body in the morning."

Jack walked with him to his car.

"Thank you again, Mister Maguire," the Doctor said. "I have been thinking all day on what you told me you witnessed and I can tell that you are going to do something about it, and if you feel that I can be of help to you, in any way, I am there. I cannot sit by and allow these people use my religion and its teaching to further their own sick ideas of how the world should be."

"That's very good of you, Doc. You have my phone number and if you can come up with anything yourself, call me."

Jack went to walk away and then turned back and said, "Oh, Doc…"

"Yes, Mister Maguire?" asked the Doctor.

"Call me Jack."

They both smiled. Jack stayed and watched him drive out of the car park; he then walked into the hospital. While he was dreading meeting his ex after she screamed down the phone at him the previous night, he was really looking forward to seeing his son.

When Jack walked into the ward, Anne was sitting with her back to the door by her son's bed. Jack could see that a lot of the tubes were gone and he looked really peaceful in his sleep. His ex spun round when she heard him coming into the room. He could see that she was ready for a fight, but when the anger soon dissipated from her face, it was as if she could see her Jack from their early days: he was bright-eyed and looked in good shape to her and she noticed that, with much relief, there was no smell of drink on him.

"How is he?" Jack asked.

"He hasn't woken up yet, but the nurse has told me that all his vital signs are getting stronger and he is breathing on his own… it looks good," she answered, in a relieved voice.

He nodded his head. She continued, "And thank you for making the effort; you look well."

Before Jack could say anything, the boy's eyes opened.

"Is that you Da?" he asked.

"It is son… and your Mother is here too," Jack answered

"How ya, Ma," Ciaran said. "Are youse fighting?"

"No son," they said in unison, while they both simultaneously held one of their son's hands, "we are not fighting."

"Well, that's great," the boy said and drifted back off to sleep.

Jack turned to his ex. "I'll stay tonight if you want. I'm not slagging, but you look like you could do with some sleep," he said softly

"Thanks, Jack. I'll be back at seven in the morning in case you've got to go off," she said, picking up her bag and walking to the door. She stopped and turned and looked at Jack sitting there holding his son's hand. *'Maybe,'* she thought to herself, *'just maybe there's a chance.'* With that, she quietly closed the door behind her.

Jack spent the best part of the night contemplating what he was going to do: he decided to contact a few old comrades from the past for a sit down and ask for their help; with all their skills combined together, Jack reckoned that he could find those responsible for the carnage and deal with them.

Eventually, Jack dozed off and dreamt he was back in the desert where the heat was unbearable and the hot sand could not be walked on with bare feet. The words that he had heard in the cyber café kept going through his mind in Arabic; they were the same words that he used to hear being chanted on a daily basis by the young men training in the desert sands. Jack's mission there was to help the Libyan trainers get these people ready to kill, as they prepared themselves for the wars that they were engaged in within their homelands.

With explosions going off around him, Jack woke with a start and he saw Anne sitting at the bed looking at him with a mug of coffee in her hand for him.

"I'm sorry," he said, "have you been here long?"

"About five minutes," she replied. "It's just after seven. Here, I got you a coffee."

"Thanks a million," Jack said, as he rose from the seat and took a mouthful of coffee. "Ah, that's great. I needed this."

She looked at him for a moment.

"You have a plan, Jack, to do something about this?"

Jack nodded his head.

"Well, be careful," she said.

"I will."

He bent over and kissed his son on the forehead.

"I'll be in touch soon," he said to her, as he walked out the door.

CHAPTER 4

After leaving the hospital, the first place that Jack headed for was the Cyber Café. Mustapha was just opening up when he walked through the door. The place was empty.

"Good morning Jack," Mustapha said. "The water off again?"

"No Mus, not this time. I want to see your CCTV footage from the other day when I was in."

"Oh, no, I cannot do that," Mustapha said, laughing nervously.

Without saying anything, Jack turned and closed the door and put the closed sign up; he then walked back over to Mustapha.

"Now my friend," he said with menace. "I really need to look at the footage from that morning."

"No, no, no Jack I cannot do that…" he said.

Jack looked him in the eye and then punched him on the nose. Jack could hear the sound of crunching bones, as blood spurted out everywhere, while

Mustapha screamed in agony. Jack then grabbed Mustapha by the hair and marched him into the office at the back of the shop.

"Now Mus, me auld flower, don't fuck me about and just give me the tape," Jack said menacingly.

"No, no please Jack… I cannot… he will be back and I will suffer greatly," Mustapha said through his tears.

"Fuck him, whoever he is, coming back. It's the here and now that you have to worry about," Jack said, as he raised his boot and kicked Mustapha in the testicles, causing him to throw up and collapse in a heap on the floor.

Jack watched Mustapha spitting up blood and sick.

"I'm going to keep doing this till you fuckin' talk," Jack said.

"Stop, stop… no more please," Mustapha pleaded.

Jack could see the TV monitors on the wall and the recording machines on the desk. He lifted Mustapha up off the floor by the hair on his head.

"Show me the day and the time that I have asked you for," he asked in a calm voice.

Mustapha's trembling hands reached and pressed a button and Jack could see the timer and the film going backwards on the old recording machine. Jack pressed the stop button when he could see himself walk in through the door. He then pressed play and he saw a group of men, including the two with the backpacks, who he instinctively knew were the group of suicide bombers. He counted seven in all and he immediately worked out that two were gone so he presumed there was going to be five more attacks.

As he studied the film intensely, he forgot about Mustapha on the floor for a split second when he caught him out of the corner of his eye reaching for the erase button. Jack's elbow smashed into Mustapha's jaw and he fell back onto the floor like a sack of potatoes, out to the world. Jack pressed the eject button and the tape popped out of the machine. "Got yehs! Yis pack of murdering little bastards," he said to himself, as he put the film into his jacket pocket and left the shop.

He knew that Mustapha would not be talking to anyone for a while, due to the state he was in, or that he would be making any complaint to the Garda. As he walked away, Jack also knew that he had to get a copy of the tape made and leave it in safe hands… and he knew the very man he had to go to, Mark Barry. Mark was a computer whiz kid from the time that computers came on the scene and before that, he was the best electronic timer maker in the IRA. He had developed the remote control firing devices that had baffled the experts of the British Army for years. Mark's biggest success was the firing devices for the homemade-mortar's that had wreaked havoc on the many British Army barracks that had been hit around Northern Ireland. Now at the age of 50, Mark had a successful computer repair shop in the IIAC shopping centre, which was in the centre of Dublin.

As soon as Jack walked into the empty shop, Mark said: "Jesus! Jack Maguire. How are yeh? Haven't seen you in years," there was a short pause. "I'm guessing there must be something serious up if you're here, right?"

Jack nodded his head. Mark went to the door and quickly locked up the shop, telling a customer who was walking into the door that he was closing for an hour.

"How are ya Mark? I have a bit of a problem that you might be able to help me out with," Jack said and he then proceeded to tell him all that had happened and what he had in his pocket.

"Fuckin' hell! Jack, I don't set eyes on you for years and you land in on top of me with this? Let me see what you have."

Jack handed him the cassette and within seconds it was playing on a monitor.

"You look like shite on that film," Mark quipped before they then watched the tape in total silence, studying everything that was on it. He stopped the film with Jack leaving the shop.

"Are they the bastards that blew up the two LUAS trains?" Mark asked.

"They are indeed. And I believe that they are not finished yet," Jack answered.

"Fuckin' hell! How can I help you Jack?" Mark asked seriously.

"Can you do me a copy of the tape and keep the original in a safe place with it to be distributed to the media if anything goes wrong for me?" Jack asked.

Mark pressed a button on a machine and there was a wiring noise.

"There, that's the copy done and I'll sort the original out, as you asked. Is there anything else I can do for you?" Mark asked.

"Can you find out where Gerry O Donnell is and send me his address to my phone?" Jack asked, giving his phone number to Mark. "I'm going around to the politicos in the office around in the square to see what they can do."

"That will be no problem getting in touch with Gerry, but good luck with that politico crowd, shower of fucks," Mark said, as he handed Jack to copy of the tape.

"You look after yourself, Jack, and remember that I am always here, if you need a hand," he said, adding, "Be careful," as Jack left the shop. Mark knew that hell was coming down the road for someone and he was glad that he was on Jack Maguire's side.

Jack made his way around the corner from the Shopping centre, towards the office of a political party in which some of his former comrades in arms were based. As he entered the building, Jack was surprised to see a reception area and even more surprised when, asking for an old friend, that the young girl behind the desk asked him to wait in a side room as the man in question, an elected Councillor, was busy and that he would be free shortly. He gave her his name, which meant nothing to her and walked into the side room. In the old days, Jack would just walk straight in, no questions asked, and just find whoever he was looking for.

As he sat there, Jack remembered that during the War there was a heavy steel door at the entrance to the building, which had a peep hole to enable the security man to checkout who was on the other side before opening up. This safety measure had been put in place after the shooting of two activists as they stood in the hallway by Loyalist extremists, while attempting to gain access to blow the building up.

'This place today was a far cry from then,' he thought to himself as he could not help notice the safe pastel colours of the walls. Jack looked around at the pictures that adorned the walls, all safe political type pictures. There was not one military type picture of Volunteers in action or any posters of prisoners' issues to tell visitors about the party's back story and how it had got to where it was at that moment. He felt well out of place and he was about to leave when two older men he knew, both now senior politicians, entered the building.

"Seamas, Martin," Jack called out.

"Jack, Jack Maguire! How are you?" Seamas asked, shaking Jack's hand weakly as Martin hurried on through the office door without saying a word, or even looking at Jack.

"What can I do for you, Jack?" Seamas asked.

"Is there somewhere that we can talk?" Jack asked.

Seamas sat down on a chair in the waiting room.

"It's a bit serious," Jack said.

"Ah, we'll be fine here," Seamas replied.

Jack quickly explained all that had gone on and about the tape that he had in his pocket. Just then, Seamas's mobile phone rang.

"Sorry about this, Jack, but I have to go upstairs for a meeting and I really don't know what I can do on this for you. I can only suggest that you bring it to the Gardaí," he shrugged.

Jack looked straight into Seamas's eyes.

"Do you know what, Seamas?" Jack said in a terse voice, "You always were a cowardly bastard during the War, who done fuck all then and you are still doing fuck all now."

With that, Jack stood up and headed out of the building. As he was walking out through the reception, the girl told him that the man he was looking for was now free to see him.

"Well you can tell him to go and fuck himself as well," Jack said over his shoulder as he left the building.

Walking down the road, Jack knew that he would have to get someone that could do something about all that the information in his possession and help him with plotting his revenge. Jack stopped into a nearby pub and although he felt a real craving for a pint, he called for a mug of coffee and thought about his next move.

There was a retired head Special Branch named Tom Duffy who Jack thought might be able to help him. Even though they had been on opposite sides, Jack had always had a grudging admiration for him for the way he treated Volunteers that he had arrested. He would never use unnecessary measures, unlike some of his colleagues who enjoyed dishing out severe beatings to captured Volunteers. In fact, Jack knew of several occasions where Tom Duffy had intervened and put a stop to such carry on and had organised medical assistance where it was needed. He thought to himself that he had nothing to lose in contacting him and seeing if he would meet for a chat.

Jack made his way back to Mark's shop in the IlAC Shopping Centre.

"How did you get on?" Mark asked.

"Shower of fuckers," Jack answered. "I couldn't get in to see the one I wanted and another, who you know well, didn't want to know," he added in disgust.

"That's the way they are these days, I told you that," said Mark. "So, what's the next move?"

"Do you remember that Special Branch man, Tom Duffy, that used to give us a hard time?" Jack asked.

"Oh, I remember that bollix," Mark recalled. "I got the digs off him and his squad several times. Well, mostly off fuckers under him."

"Have you any way of tracking him down?" Jack asked.

Mark looked at him. "Are you off the head or what?" Mark asked, as he sat down at the computer.

"That fucker retired many years ago, but I remember that he wrote a book. He gave you a few mentions in it, as I recall," Mark said, as he tapped the computer keys; within seconds the book and a photograph of Tom Duffy appeared on the screen. The back blurb of the cover stated that he had been a long serving Garda who hailed from Blessington, which was just outside Dublin. Jack watched with wonder as Mark rattled away at the computer keys.

"I'll try the phone directory for that area," Mark said and two Tom Duffy names appeared on the screen.

"Now, I'll try the electoral registrar," Mark said, more to himself; there were the two same names with addresses in that too.

"Bingo, Jack," Mark shouted, "there's your man. Look this one here has a GS beside it."

Jack remembered how the IRA would find out where the Gardaí lived years ago because the registrar had GS beside their name.

"The practice of GS beside their names stopped after some of their houses were attacked, if you recall, Jack," said Mark, "but this fella must have been too pig headed and didn't change his."

Jack scribbled down the address.

"Mark, you're the man," Jack said, slapping him on the back.

"How are you fixed for transport?" Mark asked.

"Hadn't thought… er, bus probably," Jack answered.

"The fuckin' bus? You havin' a laugh? Here take my car for a few days. It's in the car park," Mark said, throwing the keys to Jack.

"But I haven't driven in years!" Jack protested.

"If you crash, let me know and I can say it was robbed," Mark laughed.

Mark then wrote down the make and registration of the car and handed that to Jack, along with the parking ticket.

"Get on away with you now. I'll have the contact for the other lad here by the time you get back to me, two days ok?" Mark said.

"That should be sound," Jack replied.

CHAPTER 5

As Jack made his way to the car park to find the car, he realised that Mark hadn't told him which floor it was on, but rather than go back and ask, he went into the car park and it took him the best part of half an hour to find it, as he wandered from floor to floor.

He sat behind the wheel for a couple of minutes to get his bearings and get comfortable. He turned the key and the car jumped backwards in gear, nearly taking the legs off a woman carrying bags of messages.

"Here you!" she shouted. "You could have killed me there."

Jack could only apologise and drove out of there as quickly as he could. He drove slowly through the streets of the busy city, making his way south, on out into the suburb of Tallaght towards Blessington. He marvelled at the beauty of the Dublin Mountains all around him. As he drove through the small village of Blessington, he spotted the postman's van parked outside the post office with the door opened and the postman about to place a sack into it. 'That's the very man who will know where this address is,' Jack said to himself, looking at the piece of paper in his hand. He drove up alongside the van and rolled down the car window.

"Excuse me," he called out to the postman. "Can you tell me where this address is?"

"Ah, that's Tom Duffy," he said, looking at the paper. "He's only a couple of minutes from here." The postman then proceeded to give the directions to the house. "You'll probably find him out in his garden with the weather being so good," he added.

"Thanks a million," Jack said.

"Are you a friend of his?" Jack heard the postman ask as he drove away.

"Not exactly," Jack said to himself, with a smile.

Following the Postman's directions, three minutes later Jack pulled up outside a small white washed detached cottage. He sat for a few seconds, taking a deep breath before getting out of the car.

"Here goes nothing," he said out loud and walked through a small wooden gate and made his way up the garden path. The garden at the front of the house was some 50 yards long and every piece of it was subdivided into plots with all types of vegetables growing on it. At the top of the garden, beside the house, Jack saw a figure of a man bent over pulling at weeds. He stood and watched for a while. The man straightened himself every couple of minutes to rub his lower back. He had a full head of grey hair and his body looked like it had kept its youthful shape, as Jack remembered him. He wore a heavy checked shirt that was tucked into a pair of brown corduroy trousers, which were held up by a thick black belt; his working boots looked as old as the man that was wearing them.

"Isn't that a pretty picture?" Jack said.

The figure straightened up with a start and spun around. There was a look of fear for a split second in his eyes.

"I don't believe it!" the man said. "Jack Maguire! Is that you? How the fuck did you know where I live? And, more importantly, what the fuck do you want?" He asked both questions in quick succession.

"Good to see you to Tom Duffy," Jack said, enjoying the other man's discomfort, "and it's just a chat I want."

"I have nothing to chat about with the likes of you," Duffy snapped.

"I have some information that somebody has to act on straight away," Jack said, "and I think that you might be the man to do just that."

"Information... that you want to give me, is it?" Tom asked, laughing. "I never thought that I would hear those words coming from you; although I did hope it might happen at one time...You do know that I am retired?"

"I know that – and writing books as well. Do I get any money for my mention in it? But I also know that the likes of you never retire, really," Jack said.

"Feck off away from my door," Tom said. "I've plenty to be doing than to waste time talking to the likes of you…" he then added after a short pause, puzzled: "Anyway, why come to me?"

"Even though you were a bollix, and some of your methods of working were questionable, I always thought that you were a straight sort of Garda, unlike many of your colleagues," Jack said, "but if you are not interested…" he turned to walk away.

"Hold on there a minute," Tom said, his curiosity getting the better of him. "I suppose a cup of tea and a few minutes' chat never hurt anybody. Come in and don't be giving me any shite talk now."

They walked in silence into the kitchen. While putting on the kettle and getting the cups out of the press, there was an awkward silence between both men for a few minutes. Jack could see that the cottage inside could do with a good cleaning, that a woman's touch was long gone.

"No woman about the house?" Jack asked. Tom turned and looked at Jack and seemed to go into a daze.

Tom's wife, Bridget, had died suddenly two months after his retirement from the Garda. They had spent the year leading into his retirement searching for the ideal place for them to live; Bridget was the one to find their dream cottage and Tom was well pleased with her selection. They had planned to take a long holiday in the sun at first, but such was their delight with the cottage that they put the planned holiday on the back burner and got stuck into renovating the house and planning their garden.

One morning, Tom woke up early and looked out the window at the sun shining brightly in a cloudless sky, as he slipped out of bed taking care not to make any noise. He looked across at Bridget lying peacefully asleep. He got stuck into planting his new potatoes and after about an hour he went back into the kitchen to put on the kettle. He was a bit surprised that Bridget hadn't been up and about, so he tiptoed into the bedroom.

On seeing Bridget lying motionless there, he immediately sensed that something was wrong. He called out her name and got no reaction. He gently rocked her by the shoulder and still got no reaction. Tom knew that the worst had happened. Bridget had passed away in her sleep and it took many years for him to forgive God for shattering his life.

Tom snapped out of the memories of his dearly departed wife when he heard the kettle come to boil.

"No, I'm afraid not," Tom replied softly.

Pouring out the tea, he asked Jack, "Do you fancy anything stronger?"

"No, I'm making the effort to stay off it," Jack replied.

"Yeah, I heard that you had let yourself go. Drink can be an awful thing and I know from experience," Tom said, as he took a chair at the table.

Tom took a large sip of his tea.

"Now, what's going on?" Tom asked.

"Well, my young son was badly hurt on the LUAS explosion the other day," Jack started.

"Jesus, I'm sorry to hear that; is he alright?" Tom asked genuinely.

"He's coming on grand, thanks," Jack replied.

"Fuckin' Arabs… they shouldn't be allowed into the country," Tom stated with a venom that hid a story.

"It was an Arab that saved him," Jack said.

"How so?" Tom asked.

"He was the doctor at the hospital," Jack answered.

"Fuck him, sure we trained him, I'll bet," Tom said, wandering off on a rant. "There's too many of the likes of them getting in. That Minister for Justice, that Scully fella, now, he has the right idea."

"You'll always be the same Duffy, a Free State fascist," Jack said, beginning to lose his cool and getting up from the table.

"I'm a patriot, Maguire, from a long line of patriots," Tom said, staring into Jack's eyes. "For your information, my father was Tom Duffy, Staff Captain of the Cork Number One Brigade of the Irish Republican Army. He worked as a guard on the Cork train to Dublin and he used to carry dispatches for Mick Collins. He was also part of the squad that went out the day before Bloody Sunday and took out all those agents," he stated proudly.

"Your Da was out with Collins, killing police officers?!" Jack said, incredulously, sitting back down and looking at Tom.

"Those were different days," Tom said. "It was your lot that blackened the name of Republicanism."

"Oh yeah?" Jack said, enjoying the verbal battle. "Just like those Cork feckers Collins and Barry that slaughtered all around them."

47

"Ah!" exclaimed Tom. "This is going nowhere; I'm an old man with not much time left to waste, so what do you want to tell me?"

Jack took a deep breath "Those bastards that blew up the LUAS, well I know about them."

"The whole feckin' world knows about them. Sure, they made movies about what they do, the bastards. Did you not see that shite from Iraq where they cut that poor unfortunates head off in front of the cameras? Fuckin' animals," Tom said with venom. "I'd kill the lot of them."

"Tom! Tom! For fuck sake, will you listen to me?" Jack said, raising his voice. "I saw those two lunatics before they got on the LUAS, in an Internet Café."

"A what café?" Tom asked, puzzled.

"Ah! You know the ones; they're all over the place," Jack answered. "I heard them talking in Arabic and although it's been a long time for me since I heard Arabic, I could make out some words."

"What would you know about Arabic?" interrupted Tom. "You never even finished school, for feck sake."

"Let me just say, that your file on me was never complete. Twenty years ago, I spoke nothing but Arabic for a full year while I was in Libya. So, I know what I heard," Jack said.

"Twenty years ago, you say? So, that's where you disappeared to after all those soldiers were killed at that barracks in England," Tom mused. "And the whole of Britain and Ireland was out looking for you. You were our number one target at that time."

"Will you, for fucks sake, listen? I saw those two madmen and the rest of them that morning; they were inside the café when a mini bus type jeep pulled up with a driver and a passenger in it; the passenger got out and entered the café; he walked over and opened a locker where he handed out two rucksacks to two of the crowd; the rest of them got into the mini bus and the fella in the passenger seat was doing all the talking, giving out instructions. The mini bus was a big black job with a Cork registration, zero ten. It shouldn't be too hard for your lot to trace."

"Go on," said Tom, "I'm listening."

"The rest of these madmen are still out there, which means that there will be more attacks. I've seen and heard them," Jack said and then he proceeded to tell Tom about the close circuit cameras and the tape that he had from them.

"How did you get your hands on that?" Tom asked.

"Best you don't know," Jack answered, "but I'm sure that the shop owner will not be making a complaint to the Garda."

"Jesus, Jack! If what you are telling me is true, it's dynamite stuff."

"Is there anything that you can do with it though?" Jack asked.

"Indeed there is; would you be prepared to come into Garda Headquarters with me, if need be, to talk to someone?" Tom asked.

"I have no problem doing that on this issue, if it gets things moving," Jack answered.

"Give me your mobile phone number," Tom asked, getting a pen and piece of paper. Jack scribbled down his number and got up to leave.

"Time is very important here, Tom," Jack said, walking toward the door. "Here, have your crowd examine this," he said, as he left a copy of the tape on the table.

"And you'll never eat all those vegetables," Jack said over his shoulder, as he walked down the pathway to his car, looking at the garden.

"It keeps me busy," Tom shouted after him.

CHAPTER 6

Jack drove away back towards the city. It was getting dark and he phoned the hospital and spoke to Doctor Kaleem. The boy was doing fine, the Doctor assured Jack, but he asked him to stop by the hospital to see him around lunch time the next day. *'That sounds a bit strange,"* Jack thought, but he was a bit happier within himself having spoken to Tom Duffy.

Jack woke up bright and early the next morning, feeling better than he had felt in years; there was no drunken hangover and his head was clear. He showered and dressed and walked into the city centre. The request by Doctor Kaleem for him to drop into see him was a puzzle; his son was doing well so it had nothing to do with that, he mused. He stopped at a coffee shop where he ordered a black coffee and sat down at a window table. Someone had left the morning paper behind and he flicked through the pages. The Ministers for Justice and Foreign Affairs were all over the pages with the draft of new emergency legislation that the Government wanted to bring in. *"A lot of them are way over the top,"* Jack thought. *"People's civil rights are disappearing, but in the climate of fear that existed since the LUAS bombings, nobody is raising a voice of opposition."*

Jack noticed several times throughout the paper that the American stop over at Shannon airport got mentioned; the Americans seemed to be pushing their line, that to save the world from terrorism, they would need to use the Shannon facility more and more. The mention of this struck Jack as strange and it stuck in his head, but the waitress bringing his coffee over diverted his attention from the newspaper, he had some time to kill so he finished the paper, and made his way to the hospital.

It was just after 12.30 when Jack walked into the hospital canteen; he spotted the Doctor sitting on his own. He bought a coffee and made his way over to him. The Doctor stood up as Jack approached.

"Good day to you, Jack," he said. "Please take a seat, as I have something you might be interested in."

"Sounds mysterious," said Jack, as he sat down.

"Myself and some other Muslim friends were talking about all the madness that has been going on, when one of them mentioned a new young Amer who has opened a small Mosque in Cabra and was heard to be preaching pure hatred of all things Christian and Western," the Doctor said, pausing as he noticed how intense Jack was listening. "So, last evening, a group of us paid a visit to this Mosque. We entered separately and sat apart from each other. During the sermon, which was the most hate filled thing that I have ever heard, some of my friends objected to what was been said and began quoting

Allah to show another meaning to the rantings of this mad man. The Mullah began calling them traitors and infidels and he urged those sitting around the objectors to turn on them and beat them and evict them from the Mosque. As I had said nothing, I was able to sit there until the end. Never have I witnessed such violence, both verbal and physical. It was complete madness in a Mosque."

"Jesus, Doc!" Jack said excitedly. "This could be where we start. What did this fella look like?"

"I can do better than that," answered the Doc with a smile, as he took a leaflet from the inside of his jacket. "Here is a photograph of the Mad Mullah, so named by my friends and I because of all his rants against the world."

"That's our man," Jack said excitedly, "that's the fella that was standing amongst the younger ones giving the backpacks from the lockers and then I saw him sitting in the front seat of the mini bus giving the blessings to those lunatics that walked away to cause mayhem."

"Are you sure?" the Doctor asked.

"Oh, I'm sure alright; in fact, there may be a glimpse of him on the tape I have," Jack said and he proceeded to tell the Doctor where and how he had gotten the tape.

"What's our next step?" the Doctor asked.

"I am expecting a phone call in the next day or so from someone who should be in a position to put a stop to this madness," Jack said. "And with what I have and the information that you have just given me, they should be able to wrap this up quickly."

"I pray to Allah that you are right, Jack," the Doctor said.

Jack then asked the Doctor why he was getting so involved in this. The Doc looked at Jack for a moment or so.

"Jack," he said in a calm low voice, "I come from a slum refugee camp in Jordon. I was born and raised there by my parents who had been driven out of our homeland, Palestine, many years ago. We were a very poor family, we had nothing, but both my parents worked, doing all sorts of jobs to raise enough money to feed us. They saved and scrimped every penny so that they could to send me to school and college to get an education. I am the oldest of seven children and I was selected to go out into the world and save my family. Becoming a doctor was my best way of doing that. So, now I send my wages back to my parents, which has helped to educate my younger brothers and sisters and I return to the camp for two months every year to work in a medical facility that myself and others like me have set up. The outside world has the opinion that all of us Muslims are fanatics and this opinion has been shaped by similar actions all over the world like that you have witnessed here in Dublin... actions carried out by a very small group of crazed men. So, Jack, I will do whatever has to be done to help my people," the Doctor paused, "whatever has to be done," he repeated with intensity, as he rose from the table.

"You know where I am when you need me," he said and left Jack sitting there thinking over a cold cup of coffee.

CHAPTER 7

Tom Duffy sat and shook his head in amazement after Jack Maguire left him.

"What a story that was," he said to himself out loud, "but there must be something going on for him to make this effort to track me down," he continued. He searched the house until he found a mobile phone under a cushion on the sofa. "Now how do I turn you on?" he muttered. After a bit of fiddling around with the buttons, the phone came to life. "There you go now," he said to the phone, as he entered a number that was automatic in his head. After a few rings, a voice at the other end spoke.

"How are yah, Tom? Is everything alright?" the voice asked.

"I'm fine, but I would like to drop by in the morning for a chat. I think that you'll be very interested in this," Tom said.

"No problem, I'm in at ten o'clock and that's probably the best time before the day starts," the voice said.

"That's half a day over for me," Tom laughed. "See you then."

"You always were an early bird, Tom, see you so," the voice finished.

The old feelings of the chase began to flow through his veins, feelings that he hadn't felt in years, as Tom spent the next couple of hours going over all that Jack Maguire had told him, working out the how's and the what's of the story and when he had sorted most of the stuff out in his head, he knew that this was a much bigger game than the blowing up of a couple of trains in Ireland by a group of fanatics. *"Something very serious is afoot here,"* he thought.

As he retired to bed, Tom gave a wry smile with the thought that a retired Special Branch man and a retired IRA man working together, could get the answers. "And if that's the case, we are all fucked," he muttered into his pillow.

Tom was up and out at half past seven the next day to pick up a morning paper before boarding the bus in the village. There were very few passengers on at this point and, as always, he marvelled at the beauty of the county side as the bus sped towards the city and then the sense of sadness as the bus met the creeping spread of houses that seemed to get nearer to him every time he made the journey.

Reading through the paper, as he journeyed, the full extent of the proposed Law Reform bill that the Government was pushing was there to be read and, while he would have been a strong supporter of the Government, some of the things he read made him stop and think that the civil liberties brigade would have some shouting to do about most of this. They'd be particularly outraged with the proposal for compulsory ID cards for everyone in the country, with all non-Irish having their finger print on theirs. The government ministers were also planning for the deportation of certain religious leaders; the closing down of some places of worship for minority groups. Even the banning of burkas and hijabs. *'Jesus! That's all a bit strong,'* he thought.

He was also caught by the many small articles scattered throughout the paper regarding the bombings, with horrific picture to match. As he had thought the night before, this was certainly being steered in a certain direction, but for who and why, they were the questions that needed to be answered.

The bus pulled into the city centre around half past nine and Duffy walked through the city traffic towards Garda Headquarters. As he walked through the big metal gates, a voice from a sentry box to the side called out.

"Can I help you sir?" a young fresh-faced Garda asked.

"No, it's okay, I know where I'm going," Duffy replied.

"But I have to sign you in and record who you are visiting," the young Garda said.

Duffy felt more than a slight irritation rise up within himself as he fumbled through his pockets for his old ID card.

"I'm here to meet with the Assistant Commissioner, Owen Sullivan," he said, handing over his card.

The young Garda wrote down his details and handed back his card.

"You will have to go to the reception desk on the second floor, sir," the Garda said.

"I know full well where I have to go, son," Duffy retorted, as he walked away towards the entrance of the building. As he made his way through the doorway a voice rang out.

"Now, there's a man I have not seen in a few years! Tom Duffy, how are you?" Looking to his right towards the voice, Tom saw the Garda Commissioner himself walking towards him with a plain clothes Garda immediately behind him.

"Thomas Murphy. So, you are the top man these days. How are things going for you and how's the family?" Duffy asked, as they shook hands as old friends do.

"Tom, I was very sorry to hear about Bridget. I was away in America at the time, studying methods of police law enforcement, and it was always my intention to get in touch, but you know yourself how time flies by. How are you getting on? I must say that you are looking fit and well and I hear that you are growing the best vegetables in Wicklow?" the Commissioner asked playfully.

"Thanks for that, Thomas, there was so many people there that I don't remember any of it. As for the vegetables, I'm just filling in time," Tom Duffy answered.

"What do we owe the pleasure of the visit?" the Commissioner asked, turning to his sidekick. "This here is the one and only Tom Duffy, a living legend in the force."

"I am very pleased to meet you sir," the sidekick said respectfully and with a strong handshake.

Tom nodded back to him.

"I'm here to have a chat with Owen Sullivan," Tom replied. The slightest frown came over the Commissioner's face, Tom noticed. Turning to his sidekick, he instructed him to get Tom's phone number and gave him his card.

"I have to fly, Tom, with all the stuff that's going on. I have to meet now with the Cabinet to give them an up-to-date on where we are, which is nowhere, I can tell you. We haven't a clue and that's the truth. It's great to see you, my friend. I'll drop over for some spuds off you soon," the Commissioner said, as he walked out the door.

Stepping out of the lift at the second floor, Tom approached the Reception desk with his ID card in his hand.

"I'm here to see Owen Sullivan," he said. The Garda manning the desk was another fresh-faced female Garda straight out of the college, Tom thought to himself. She looked down through a list of names in front of her.

"Ah yes, there you are, sir," she said. "Would you care to take a seat for a few minutes, the Assistant Commissioner is running a few minutes late this morning. Can I get you a tea or coffee?" she asked.

"No thanks, I'm fine," Tom answered, taking a seat. Within minutes the lift opened and out stepped

Owen O' Sullivan with two assistants in toe. Tom had to blink his eyes several times at the sight of the Assistant Commissioner – gone was the young Owen O'Sullivan that he remembered as a hard working fit-looking detective whose only downfall back then was perhaps being a bit too eager to impress his superiors. But his eagerness backfired when he led that disastrous operation, funnily enough, thought Tom, against Jack Maguire. Standing in front of him now was a slightly overweight man who either took a lot of holidays in the sun or spent a lot of time on a sun bed, so tanned was he. He was immaculately groomed with not a hair out of place and both his shirt and trousers had razor sharp pleats in them and his expensive looking black leather shoes had the appearance of being spit and polished, Tom thought, but not by the wearer. So great was the shine off them, Tom joked to himself that he could almost see the reflection of his face. As they shook hands, Tom could not help notice how soft the skin was and how manicured the nails were.

"Good morning, Tom," he said. "Come with me, one of yis get a pot of tea for two and a few nice biscuits," he ordered. "One of the benefits of the job, Tom, you don't have to make your own tea."

The Assistant Commissioner walked behind a massive desk that looked out over the city and had a battery of phones of all colours on it. He invited Duffy to take a seat and they engaged in idle chitchat until the tea arrived and they were left alone.

"Now, Tom, what can I do for you?" the Assistant Commissioner asked.

"Well, Owen, this is a strange one," Tom said and he proceeded to tell him of the visit from Jack Maguire and all that he had said.

"My God, Tom, but that is some tale," the Assistant Commissioner said. "You do know, Tom, that this Maguire fella has been hitting the bottle for years?"

"Yes, Owen, I've been aware of that, but this somehow seems different and here is the DVD from the Internet café that he spoke of."

The Assistant Commissioner pressed a button on his desk and a drawer opened with a DVD player in it; he placed the disc in it and a large television screen on the wall flickered into life. They both watched as Jack Maguire entered the Internet café.

"By Jesus, he looks in bits," the Assistant Commissioner said. Duffy said nothing. The Assistant Commissioner was beginning to irritate him with his attitude to the whole thing. He noticed the young Arabs rattling away in Arabic, just as Jack had said, but he also noticed that on two occasions Jack stopped and slightly turned towards the line of Arabs. They watched as Maguire left the shop and Duffy could make out a black van type jeep pull up outside.

"Owen, do you have anybody in the building that speaks Arabic?" Duffy asked.

"Tom," the Assistant Commissioner said, "don't tell me that you are taking all this seriously? This looks to me like the ramblings of a drunkard, looking for attention."

"Please just humour me. Can you get someone who speaks Arabic?"

"Okay. We should have someone, hang on a second," he answered and pressed another button. "Can you ask for someone in Immigration that can speak Arabic to get in here immediately," he ordered.

They spent the next few minutes discussing the for and against of the story when the office door opened and a middle eastern man was ushered in. The Assistant Commissioner explained what was going on and stressed the confidentiality of the discussion and replayed the DVD. The man watched and listened intently and then turned ashen-faced to the Assistant Commissioner.

"Sir! They are talking about making the ultimate sacrifice, see here," he pointed to the screen, "they are congratulating these two, who have been selected to go first," he said in a hushed voice.

"So, Maguire is right!" Duffy stated. "And that means that there are probably five more to go."

"Tom, I cannot thank you enough for what you have brought in; leave it with me now and we'll get cracking on it," the Assistant Commissioner said, as he rose from his desk, looking at his watch.

Duffy felt that he was being rushed out the door of the office.

"Thanks again, Tom," the Assistant Commissioner said and before he knew it, he was back out on the street having been escorted there by the young Garda from the reception desk.

*

The Assistant Commissioner stood and looked out the window at Duffy slowly walking out the gate.

"People have paid big money for this view," he said to himself. He thought back to his times working under Tom Duffy, firstly on the streets of Dublin and then in the Special Branch all over the country. He recalled one time in particular when they had surrounded a house in the country that he had received information that Jack Maguire was holed up in. He had been put in charge of a squad of men whose main brief was to capture Maguire. He had made a big deal of this operation to his bosses and his media friends were alerted to what was about to happen. All was ready for his big moment until the squad, led by him, burst into the house only to find it empty. The fire was still lit and a half-finished meal and a hot cup of tea sat on the table. They could not have missed him. "Pull the place apart," he recalled shouting out loud until one of his men found an open trapdoor in the bathroom, which led to an escape tunnel. He had been made look a right fuckin' eejit. He knew that his chances of ever getting the top job in the force was gone. The media had a field day on him, he remembered, and none of it was good. O'Sullivan snapped out of his thoughts.

"I could have been Commissioner by now, only for that day," he said out loud. And now Maguire was back to upset the years he had spent clawing his way over people to get to where he stood now. While he had not got the big job, he had done well padding his bank account and setting himself up for a lucrative afterlife on retirement from the Garda, thanks to his good relationship with the Minister and his pal in the American Embassy.

He turned and lifted a red phone off the desk and dialled a number, within seconds a voice answered at the other end.

"I'm afraid that we have a bit of a problem that has just cropped up," he said and proceeded to tell all that had gone on with Tom Duffy. There was a long pause at the other end of the phone.

"Are you there?" he asked.

"Of course I am fuckin' here," the voice said, "and you better deal with it. Just fuckin' deal with it."

The Assistant Commissioner sat at his desk for a few moments and then called one of his assistants into the office.

"I have a job for you, nobody but you and I are to be privy to it, do you understand?" he asked.

"Yes sir, I understand," the assistant said obediently.

"I want you to get me all the information you can on a fella called Jack Maguire; he used to be a top Provo back in the day when they were the main threat to this country… fairly high up with that crowd. And also the same on the man who was just in here with me, a former head of the Special Branch, Tom Duffy. And I will again stress that this has to be kept extremely tight."

He thought that perhaps he should also have a couple of his journalist friend on stand-by if it was required to launch a black propaganda campaign on this.

When his assistant left the office, he sat down at his desk and looked out the window again over the city.

"This is all I fucking need at this time," he moaned.

CHAPTER 8

Duffy walked back through the city towards his bus stop, wondering if he had achieved anything by meeting the Assistant Commissioner. What was clear to him now was that Jack Maguire was on the ball with his information and that more deaths, for sure, were on the way if nothing was done. He rang Jack's phone as he walked and after a couple of rings Jack answered with a question.

"Well, how did things go for you?" he asked.

"Strange, very strange… all that you outlined to me is definitely the real deal," Tom said. "We had an Egyptian translator with us going over the dialogue on the DVD and you are right about what was going on."

"And the strange bit?" Jack asked cautiously.

"Well, I got the impression that the man I brought the DVD to was not that keen on doing anything."

"What the fuck do you mean, not keen on doing anything?" Jack asked, his voice rising with anger.

"I can't put my finger on it, but my gut feeling is telling me that something is not right," Tom replied.

There was a silence from Jack's end of the phone for several seconds.

"What are you saying to me, Tom?" Jack asked in a slow deliberate voice.

"I'm saying, that for the moment, there does not seem to be a great deal that I can do to help you with all that you have uncovered," Tom said dejectedly.

"Well, Tom," Jack said, "I think that you know by now that I cannot let this go and that I must act on this."

"Yes, I do know Jack," Tom replied in a voice that as much as suggested that Jack should maybe carry on his own investigation using his own methods. Tom knew full well that he was giving Jack the go ahead and that more than likely illegal methods of gaining the right information would be used. He finished the phone call by saying that he would be back in touch within a couple of days.

While on the bus on the way home, Duffy thought of the few words he'd had with the Commissioner, Tom Murphy. He felt about through his pockets and found the card that the young fella with the Commissioner had given him. He looked at the card. "If I hear nothing within the next two days, I'll give this number a call," he said to himself.

*

Jack spent the next day following Tom Duffy's phone call, trying to work out why Duffy had as much as told him that he'd get more results getting to the bottom of what was going on doing things his own way. He'd been up to the hospital to visit his son several times and each time the Doctor would fill him in on his son's progress and on the growing feeling amongst the Muslim population in Dublin that this lunatic group were not finished.

Jack had re-established the link by phone with his business partner in the Security firm they had and he visited the clubs in Temple Bar, which they looked after. The biggest and most popular one was a club which was front door secured by a team led by a Croatian lad named Stan.

Stanislav Sosabowski was an ex elite squad Croatian Army veteran from the war that savaged his homeland. He moved to Ireland after been demobbed from the army following the civil war. He found that the skills that had been drilled into him were no longer needed. A friend of his had introduced him to Jack's partner and he got work immediately. Stan then enrolled in night college to learn English and settled down well in Dublin. Over the next couple of years, he sent home money weekly to his parents; he also saved up enough to bring his younger sister to Dublin and enrol her in college. His sister Anita stayed with him in his apartment and most Friday nights she and a couple of her new friends from college would come to the club in Temple Bar where he worked and he would make sure that they got in for free; this enabled him to keep a 'big brother' eye on her.

Stan, along with all the other lads, had sent his support to Jack when he heard that his son had been hurt. While on his visit, Jack thanked them for their support and, as the queue to gain admission to the club was building up, he left the lads to it and carried on with his tour.

*

Stan waved goodbye to Jack and noticed two fellas in the queue with trainers and hoodies on; he knew that they would be going nowhere, just behind them a fella on his own caught his eye, black curly hair, middle eastern look and well-dressed, but before he could think any more of why he had caught his attention, the two hoodies were at the door.

"I'm sorry my friends, but we cannot allow you in tonight," Stan said politely.

"Why the fuck not?" one of the hoodies said threateningly, as he leant into Stan's face.

"The club policy is that no trainers or hoodies allowed," Stan replied calmly.

"Fuck this, no foreigner is stopping me get into a club in my own town," the second hoodie said, while throwing a punch in Stan's direction.

But Stan had been watching the guy out of the corner of his eye and was ready. In a split second, number two hoodie was on his stomach on the ground with his arm up his back and Stan's knee pressing on the back of his neck.

"Ah here, leave it out," number one hoodie shouted. "Let him up out of that, we're only out for a laugh," he pleaded, but with no thought of jumping in to help his mate.

Within a minute the incident was over, the two hoodies left the doorway but waited till they were a good few yards away before shouting threats and abuse at Stan, as is the way of cowards, Stan thought. The middle eastern looking guy who had caught Stan's eye that was on his own in the queue had gone into the club while he had been busy. "I'll have to go and find him," Stan said to himself, as he felt uneasy about him. Just then, his sister came to the door.

"Hello big brother," she greeted him in Croatian. "I have brought you and your friends some sandwiches for your break."

Stan and his two partners thanked her and ushered her and her friends through the crowd into the club.

"Jaysus, Stan, I always look forward to these sandbos late at night," one of his fellow doormen said. This distracted Stan for a few minutes from going and searching for the guy with the black curly hair who had slipped into the club while Stan had been dealing with the two hoodies.

The black curly head guy was now standing in the middle of the dance floor, looking around him at the flashing lights, the loud music and the scantily dressed women. One of the young women walked over to him and began dancing in front of him. He smiled. "Come on, come you harlot," he said inwardly, as she moved in closer and put her arms around his neck. The last thing she heard was his voice in her ear and her last sight was his hand raised with a wire going down his sleeve. An almighty explosion ripped through the club with such force that the three men at the door were blown across the street.

Outside, Stan instinctively knew that it was a bomb. Stan's military training kicked in. He rolled to his side quickly feeling all parts of his body; there was no blood, but he could hear nothing, he knew that this would pass. He got to his feet and lifted his two workmates up, they were both ok.

His sister! He scrambled through the debris and smoke into the burning club where a scene of complete devastation met him. There were bodies scattered everywhere. Stan began to hear the wail of sirens, but worse than that he could hear the screams of people. He could feel his two mates behind him and they began carrying out bodies of people, not sure if they were dead or alive. After what seemed like an age, some Gardaí arrived on the scene.

Stan was working on automatic mode carrying people out when he got a shout for one of his mates. He dreaded making his way over to him through the rubble and then he saw his sister was half buried beneath a pile of bricks; her face had been left intact but the back of her head was gone. They worked feverishly to get her out from under the rubble. Stan lifted her up in his arms and let out an animal-like scream, "Nooooooo!"

He cried as he walked out over the rubble, carrying her to an ambulance.

*

Jack heard the explosion and was running back to the club when, after about 50 yards or so, he had to stop to catch his breath. He leaned against a wall.

"Fuck this," he said out loud and began running again. He got even less distance this time when he had to stop again. He could see that there was total mayhem outside the club, but leaning against the wall trying to catch his breath meant that he was of no use to anyone.

Making his third attempt to reach the club, he got there and the first person he met was one of his lads who told him about Stan's sister. Stan was refused an Ambulance for her as she was already confirmed dead and he was told they were only taking people who were alive and injured to the hospital. The paramedics had kicked the door in of a pub nearby that was closed and they had begun laying out the dead bodies in there.

"Jack," he said, "there are loads of them."

Jack made his way into the pub where the bodies were laid out and found Stan sitting cradling his sister's head in his arms.

"Jack I saw him," he cried. "I saw the bastard that did this… and I did nothing about it."

"Take it easy, Stan, and tell me what happened," Jack said.

"I saw this guy on his own in the queue, eastern looking with black curly hair and I sensed that something was not right but before I could confront him this happened… look what they have done to my sister, Jack," Stan sobbed.

"Stan, I need you now, before the Garda close off the scene, to come with me and show me where the office is with the close circuit television recorders are," Jack said.

Stan looked at him with dead eyes.

"Now!" Jack ordered in a hard voice, which snapped Stan into life.

They quickly made their way through the rubble, ignoring the shouts from the firemen and Garda that were present. There were no lights, but Stan knew his way to the office at the back of the club. The manager of the club lay dead in the doorway of the office. Jack quickly stepped over him. Stan stood at the door over the manager, while Jack looked for the recorder. He took the tape out of it and stuffed it into his inside pocket. They both then took hold of the manager's body and carried him out.

"Are you two mad? Did you not hear me telling you to stop?" a Garda shouted at them as they emerged. "Nobody's allowed in there."

"We work here and we knew that the manager was in the back office," Jack said. "Unfortunately, we could do nothing."

The Garda looked down at the body, turned away and was sick.

"It's a disaster," the Garda said, as he turned aside again and threw up all that had been in his stomach for a second time. They carried the body to where the rest were laid out and Jack stayed with Stan and the men for the rest of the night. They did all that they could to help the injured. Jack estimated that there were 60 dead and hundreds injured.

As dawn was breaking, the Garda Superintendent in charge walked over to Jack.

"I know that you are Jack Maguire and I want to thank you and your men for the Trojan work that you did here tonight."

Turning to Stan, the Garda Superintendent said, "My sympathy goes to you and your family on the loss of your sister. These are terrible times that we are living in."

As he walked away, Jack said his farewells to the two lads, telling them to go home and get some rest. He held Stan's hand in a firm handshake and told him to stay with his sister and that he would ring him later in the day.

CHAPTER 9

After saying goodbye to Stan, Jack walked over the half penny Bridge towards the north side of the city. He stopped half way and looked back – everywhere leading into Temple Bar was sealed off with the Garda tape. He felt a raw rage building up inside him. It was now eight o'clock and the city was beginning to awaken. He rang Tom Duffy and when he answered the phone, Jack exploded.

"You useless shower of bastards," he began. "I've just left a scene of 60 people dead and hundreds injured with limbs blown off. I fuckin' told you that this would happen and youse did fuck all with my information. So fuck youse; I'm doing things my own way from here on."

After this rant, Jack then turned off the call in anger before Tom could talk and switched his phone onto silent mode.

Jack made his way to Mark Barry's shop, hoping that it would be opened. Mark was pulling up the shutters as he arrived.

"Jaysus, Jack! Have you had a look at yourself?" Mark asked. Jack took a look at his reflection in a window; his clothes and hair were covered in dust and he could see that his hands were cut and scraped from lifting the rubble all night; there was also large patches of dried blood on his clothes.

"I've been in the club that was blown up last night," Jack said.

"What club? I've heard no news this morning," Mark replied.

"They've struck again, the LUAS madmen," Jack said, "over 60 people killed and a couple of hundred injured."

"Come in and get cleaned up," Mark said. "I'll see what's out the back clothes-wise, that might help you out."

"You can help out with this Mark," Jack said, handing over the tape. "This is the close circuit tape from the club. I'm particularly interested in the queue outside for the 10 to 15 minutes before the explosion."

"That should be no problem, Jack," Mark said, walking back from the storeroom with some clothes. "Here try these auld jeans on and here's a windbreaker jacket. There is also a bathroom out the back; throw some water over your head and I'll get started on this tape."

Jack took the clothes and thanked him.

"I almost forgot," Mark continued, "I have something else to show you. I've done individual photographs of that crew in the internet café... have a look when you are ready."

Jack stripped off the dirty clothes and buried his face in his cupped hands of cold water. He then threw the cold water over his head, drying himself off with an old cloth he found. He put the jeans on, which were a size too big, and also the windbreaker jacket, which was also a bit big, but he felt better with the wash and change. He then began looking through the photographs.

"These are brilliant Mark," Jack said. "These two here are the pair that I saw putting on the backpacks. So, we can draw an x across them; that leaves these five. Now let's see the club tape?"

They spent the next hour slowly going over the tape. They could see Stan and the other lads marshalling the queue; they watched as Stan dealt with the two hoodies and saw a young girl give Stan a package.

"That's Stan sister, Mark," Jack said, sadly. "She got killed. Four minutes later the explosion happened and the tape flickered out."

"Let's go back ten minutes on the tape," Jack suggested, "the only disturbance of the night was the two hoodies."

They slowly scanned the queue leading up to that moment. Jack noticed a guy on his own behind the hoodies and when the row kicked off, the guy paid no attention to it, unlike everyone else. He just walked quickly into the club.

"Can you freeze the tape on that guy there?" Jack asked, pointing to a black curly haired dark skinned guy.

"This one here?" Mark asked, bringing the face into full view. Jack looked at the still photographs in his hand.

"That's the bastard," Jack shouted, pointing to the still photo and then the screen.

"You're right there, Jack," Mark agreed, looking at both screen and photo.

Jack drew an x over the photo.

"Now there are four of those madmen left," Jack stated as he gathered up the photographs and headed for the door.

"I almost forgot, Jack," Mark said, "I contacted Donegal Phil for you and he said that he would be here in Dublin this afternoon. He said that he would see you in the little pub on the corner at Busarus in store street around four o'clock."

"That's great, Mark, thanks," Jack said. "I'll see him there. Do you want your car back yet?"

"No, no hold onto it for a few days more," Mark said. "And Jack, don't forget that I'm here whenever you need me. And be careful out there."

"I know that, Mark. I'd be lost without you so far. What you're doing with these tapes is a massive help. Thanks," Jack said and walked out the door.

Outside, Jack looked at his phone and noticed three missed calls from Tom Duffy. "Fuck him!" he said to himself, as he made his way home to his flat for a few hours' sleep.

It was early afternoon when he woke up from a fitful sleep. He showered and dressed and sat down with a cup of tea in his hand to gather his thoughts. There were now six missed calls from Tom Duffy on his phone. Jack knew that he would have to ring him back at some stage, but first he rang Stan and asked him how he was. Stan immediately asked Jack for a meeting as soon as possible. He looked across at the clock on the mantelpiece, it said one o'clock. Jack agreed to meet up with Stan at half past two at a hotel in the city centre. Jack then rang Tom Duffy who immediately let rip at Jack.

"Don't you ever shout and roar down the phone at me again or we are finished," Tom said. "I know that things are not right and that something stinks to the high heaven, but if this thing is to be tackled, you need me!" he said.

"Your right Tom," Jack said. "I had spent the night at that club. One of my lads off the door, his sister was killed and me head was away with it," Jack said, almost apologizing.

There was silence as they both calmed down after a few seconds.

"I'll be up in the city tomorrow morning and I'll see you in Wynne's hotel on Abbey street around eleven o'clock," Tom said.

"That will do," Jack replied, "see you there."

CHAPTER 10

In a small room in the bowels of the American Embassy, three men sat around a table. Two of the men were Americans, one being roughly ten years older than the other, both were dressed in sharp dark blue suits, white shirts and dark blue ties. The older man gave off an air of complete calmness while the younger man had a habit of over emphasizing his importance in the room. The third man was an out of shape, shabbily dressed Irish Government Minister who found himself, at that moment, way out of his depth in the company of the two Americans. The room was bare of all furniture other than the wooden table and three chairs, the Irish Minister found himself sitting on his own across from the other two. The single light with its dimness and no windows letting in natural light all combined to add to the Irish Minister's uncomfortable demeanour.

"This has gone too far," the Irish Government Minister said. "There is serious pressure coming from everyone around the Cabinet table to get a grip on what is happening."

"What's happening is that you are losing your balls, that's what's happening," the Undersecretary to the American Ambassador stated.

"Who the fuck do you think you are talking to like that? There are Irish people being killed here," the Minister exclaimed.

"Listen to me very carefully, Minister," the Yank said in a slow deliberate voice, "when you were caught in bed with that underage hooker in Washington and we saved your skin and when you took that large wad of money from the company that transport our troops through Shannon airport, you had no thought for the Irish people and that was the moment that meant that I could talk to you in whatever manner I want."

"Steady on there boys," the third voice said with authority, "there is no need for this sort of talk, cool heads are what's needed at this moment. Now Minister, you say that we may have a side problem that has cropped up, please explain?"

"I got a call regarding an ex-Provo and an ex-head of Special Branch combining to tackle our Muslim friends. It seems that the Provo's son was hurt in the LUAS explosion and he stumbled upon the boyos who done it, before they set out. He is not a happy man and his past record shows that he is quite capable of doing a lot of damage," the Minister concluded, still visibly upset with the comments from the Undersecretary.

"And the ex-Special Branch man?" the third man asked.

"Well, he believes that the Provo has the information and the where with all to get involved in a serious way, but he is looking for Garda Headquarters to act on it," the Minister answered.

"Our man in Garda Headquarters is still ok with us, isn't he?" the third man asked.

"Oh yes, he's sound," the Minister replied.

"Good then, this mission is nearly complete, so have him keep those two on the long finger for a while longer and everything will be fine."

The Minister stood up.

"Leave that with me, Mr Ambassador," he said and turned, ignoring the Undersecretary as he walked out.

"You know your way out then," the Undersecretary shouted after him.

"You'll have to stop winding that guy up, Bob," the Ambassador chided.

"He's an asshole," the Undersecretary replied.

"Yes – but he's our asshole. And for now we need him on board. Have our observation teams intensify their work and also put them on those two, Duffy and Maguire as well. Make sure that they are on 24-hour watch. We are nearly there and I do not want any fuck ups, do you understand?" the Ambassador said.

"I understand fully, sir," the Undersecretary said.

The Minister made his way to his Merc in the Embassy car park; his driver was sat behind the wheel reading the racing pages of the morning paper. The

Minister dropped into the back seat, cursing to himself.

"I have the word on a couple of winners going today, if you fancy a bet," the driver said.

"A bet?" the Minister shouted. "A fucking bet! The world is about to collapse around me and you are more interested in the fuckin' horses?! Get me out of here."

The driver looked in his rear view mirror. 'My Jaysus, he looks well rattled,' he said to himself, wondering what could have happened in the Embassy, as he drove away out the gates.

The Minister was in deep thought as the car drove through the traffic back to Government Buildings. *The nerve of that fucker talking to me like that,'* he thought. *'One little indiscretion in Washington and that bollix thinks that he owns me. Well, we'll see about that.'* He decided that he would direct his senior Garda contacts to begin a dirty campaign against the American Ambassador's Undersecretary with the aim of catching him in a compromising position, then the tables would be turned.

"Yes," the Minister said to himself, feeling better within, "that's what we'll do."

The car pulled up at government buildings.

"Here," he said to his driver, throwing him four 50 euro notes. "Put that on those tips that you have."

He got out of the car. *Things might not be so bad after all,'* he thought, as he skipped up the steps to his office.

CHAPTER 11

Tom dug out the card with the Commissioner's Aide's name and number on it. He rang the number and after two rings it was answered.

"Hello," the voice at the other end said.

"This is Tom Duffy here, you gave me your number the other day when I met the Commissioner."

"Ah, yes, Mr Duffy, how can I help you?" he asked.

"Well, I have a handle on the horrific events of the past week and I seem to be getting stonewalled within the force with it. Is it possible that I could catch the Commissioner in the morning for a quick chat? I've to be in the city for 12, if it's possible to fit me into his schedule?" Tom asked.

"I don't see a problem with an early call. Let me ring you back with a time; it could be this evening when I can ring you back," the Aide said.

Tom spent the next few hours pulling up weeds with a frustrated temper, reflecting on the situation that he found himself in; his initial feeling on his meeting with the Assistant Commissioner was bearing true – he had been a useless bastard when he had served in the Special Branch, he recalled, but why would he not act on the information that he'd been given? That was the question and it could only be that he had something to gain or lose, but what? That was another question Tom needed answering.

Within a few hours, there wasn't a weed left in the whole garden. Tom felt a bit better when he had finished and strolled down to the village for a paper. The woman in the shop bid him a good day and was full of talk about the awful events of the night before in the city. Tom bought two papers, which was a surprise to the woman as she never knew him to buy even one. He said his good byes to her and made his way back to the house where he put the kettle on and made a cup of tea. He then sat down to read the papers. It was about mid-afternoon when a big dark blue car pulled up outside his house. Tom peeped out through the curtains. "Two visitors in as many days!" he said out loud to himself. "It's getting like the city centre here," he added.

Two men got out of the car and walked quickly up the pathway. Tom could not make out who they were, but he noticed a third one left sitting in the driver's seat. He went and opened the door.

"Jesus, tonight!" he said. "Commissioner Thomas Murphy! What has you here at this time of day?" he asked surprised. "Come in, come in."

"Tom, I got a call from David here after you rang him and my curiosity could not wait till tomorrow," the Commissioner said.

"Sit down, the pair of you, would you like a drop of tea?" Tom asked.

"Not for me, sir" David said.

"Nor me, Tom. Time is short and I know that you didn't call David here just to have tea," the Commissioner said.

Tom got straight down to business, outlining all that he had: his visit from Jack Maguire; his calling in to see the Assistant Commissioner Sullivan; the use of the Arab interpreter; and Maguire's phone call that morning. He also told how Sullivan had held onto the tape and his feeling of been shunted out of his office.

The Commissioner looked at his aide when Tom finished.

"I told you that this man would have something crucial to tell us on the way out here," he said

"You did indeed, sir," the aide replied.

"I'm sure you will have worked out in your head, Tom, which is the best way forward?" the Commissioner asked.

"I have, but maybe its best that you are not in the room when I talk about it," Tom suggested to the Commissioner, who immediately understood what Tom was saying.

"Maybe I should throw my eye over these vegetables of yours that I have heard so much about, for a few minutes" the Commissioner said.

"Take some of the best spuds in Wicklow and a head of cabbage for yourself," Tom offered, as the Commissioner left the room.

"Now," said Tom to David, leaning forward in his chair as he proceeded to outline to him how and why Jack Maguire should be supported in his operation, that he believed that Maguire would find these lunatics and kill every last one of them. He stated that he also believed that Jack Maguire would get to the bottom of who was really behind all of this and why.

"You do know, of course, that allowing a group of men carte blanch to kill people is illegal," David said.

"Of course I do, that's why, he," he said, pointing out to the Commissioner, "is out there picking vegetables and we are having this discussion, which incidentally never took place."

"I will be of whatever assistance that I can," David said. "You said that you could be up in the city tomorrow, mid-afternoon for us to have a chat?" he asked.

"Yes, I will see you in Bewley's coffeehouse in Grafton street at that time," Tom agreed. "That will do for now – before he takes all my vegetables on me!" he added as he went to find a plastic bag for the Commissioner.

"These look good," he said as he put the potatoes and a head of cabbage in the bag.

"Have you left me anything?" Tom asked.

"You've enough here to see you through two winters. I'll have to come back out to you Tom," the Commissioner said, as he turned to David. "Everything look good?" he asked.

"Yes, indeed, sir; we are all on the one road," he replied.

"Good man, all the best for now, Tom... although I have a feeling in me waters that we will be talking again soon," the Commissioner said, as he walked briskly down the pathway. Both men turned and waved at Tom as they got into the car and drove away.

The adrenalin began to flow through the Commissioner's veins now that he believed they would get somewhere. The Commissioner turned to his aide when they got comfortable in the car.

"Well David, what did you think of all that?" he asked.

David put his finger to his lip in a shush motion and opened a small hard backed case that was on the floor. He took out a handheld scanner and turned it on, after a minute of waving it around, he stopped.

"The car is clear of bugging devices, sir," he said. "Do you know Tom Duffy well?"

"I do, he was my boss in the Special Branch for many years and a smarter, craftier, more honest man you could never meet. Tom was never into the politics of the job and as such made enemies for himself within the force and so when his age said retirement, he got the elbow. So, if Tom says that Jack Maguire is on to something, then it's for real. Maguire was our number one target for Republican terrorist activity for many years, but he was clever enough to give us the slip so many times."

"The brick wall that Tom has come up against is Sullivan," David stated, "and we know that he is rotten to the core, but in my opinion there is someone behind him and it can only be at

Government level. He hasn't the brain for this scale of thing, sir."

"David," the Commissioner said, after several moments of deep thought, "give Tom Duffy all the support he needs. Use your connections to find out who is in charge of the bombing investigation – and I don't mean the public face of who is in charge, but who it is exactly that has the final shout on what goes on. Stuff will happen, if I know Maguire's form, and we must be ready to deal with the fallout."

"Very well, sir," David said and they both sat back with their thoughts as the car sped back towards the city with the evening darkness beginning to descend.

David looked across the car at the Commissioner and thought that he had never seen him look so troubled in all the years that he had served with him. He reflected on his career in the force to date, as the car glided silently along. His parents had been set against him joining the Garda, as his father was a sitting high court judge and his mother was a successful barrister. So, the legal life had been mapped out for him from his early days in university, but he always felt within himself that the he had a different role to play in life and he seen that the Gardaí were at the coalface of the world that his parents were so fully integrated in. Because of his seemingly privileged background, the training for him, in the Garda Recruitment Centre, was made extra hard from some of the instructors and from some of the recruits, but with the drive that was within him, he excelled on all fronts, becoming top of his class and with his knowledge of different languages acquired through his school days, he was more than capable of meeting the needs of the modern day Garda. He had risen through the ranks from uniformed Garda on the street, to plain clothes detective in a couple of years and unknown to him at that time, some members of the senior ranks were keenly watching his progress.

The morning that he got the phone call from the then Chief Superintendent Thomas Murphy to come to his office in Garda Headquarters was the changing point of his life. He had known full well of the work and career of the Chief Superintendent from his studies in the training college and the tales that were around the Garda stations that he served in and when he was asked that morning to join the Chief Superintendent's staff, he did not have to think twice. Now he was the main aide to Thomas Murphy, the Garda Commissioner, and as such his powers were far reaching. He ran the Armed Response Units, which had been his brainchild to combat the rise in professional crime that had begun to sweep the country; their brief was to strike immediately at reported crime and to hit the criminals before they committed offences. He was also involved in the formation and training of the Government Ministers security teams.

The present problem of fanatical attacks on the people of the country was one that he nor anybody else had foreseen, but looking again across the car at the Commissioner and knowing the faith that he had in Tom Duffy, he felt more than confident that they could deal with what was coming at them.

'This Jack Maguire is an interesting addition to the fight,' he thought. Having checked out his background history, he could see the problems that past

departments of the Garda **Síochána** had in trying to capture him – and with his skills in the present fight, David agreed with Tom Duffy's assessment of how things should go forward.

CHAPTER 12

Jack had a busy day ahead; from mid-morning on, he had meetings arranged, so he made his way to the hospital early. He walked into the ward where his son was and he was delighted to see him sitting up in the bed reading a comic.

"Howya, Da," the boy said with delight. "You're early."

"Howya, son," Jack replied, tussling his boy's hair. "You look in great form today."

"Yeah, I'm feeling good... just a bit sore in me head though."

"That will pass, just take it easy," Jack advised him.

"Me Ma was up last night and she brought me these comics, I think that she still thinks that I'm still a kid," the lad said.

"Yeah, she probably forgot that you are 12," Jack laughed. Just then Doctor Kaleem entered the ward.

"How are you, Jack?" he asked.

"I'm grand… and how is this little fellow getting on?" Jack asked.

"I think that he can go home in a couple of days," the Doctor stated.

"That's great news! Isn't it son?"

"Will you be coming home with me Da?" the lad asked, quietly.

"I'll have to have a chat with your Ma about that," Jack replied, "but I promise that you will see a lot more of me. I'll see you again in the morning son, I have to go and talk with the good Doctor here."

"Ok, Da, see you then," the lad said, as he got back into reading his comics.

The Doctor led Jack into a small office that was empty.

"No-one will interrupt us in here," the Doctor said.

"Here's the situation, Doc," Jack began, taking the photos out of his inside jacket pocket, "these are the guys from the internet café," and he then paused to point out the ones with the X's on them, "these two are the ones from the LUAS bombs and this one here is the one from the night club, the rest of them are still out there."

"I have been spending time at that Mosque and I have definitely seen those ones there," the Doc said, pointing at photographs with no X's on them. "They always stay behind when the rest of us go home after prayers."

"I'll come with you this evening, if you don't mind, Doc. I'll be able to follow them to where they are staying and then we will find out where their nest is."

"Yes, good thinking."

"I'll meet you at the gates of the big Catholic Church in Phibsboro at seven."

The Doc answered without hesitation: "I'll be there, see you then."

They shook hands.

"Catch you later," Jack said, as he left the small office.

Jack felt quite good leaving the hospital: his son was in great shape, fit enough to go home, and he felt that he was closing in on those responsible for putting him there. His son asking him if he was going home with him threw him a bit; he really would have to sit down with his mother and talk, really talk, about their son away from the courts and legal people. He knew that he hadn't had much feeling for her for a number of years, but he could now see what a useless bastard he had been to her. *'Maybe,'* he thought, *'given a chance, things could turn out a bit different.'* He could still recall the good times they had together in their halcyon days.

It was a fine morning as he walked into the city to the hotel to meet Stan as arranged. On the way, he diverted to Moore Street to one of the many mobile phone shops that now ran the length of the street. "This is definitely not the Moore Street that I knew," he said to himself. Nearly all the fruit stalls that ran along both sides of the street were gone and now only a couple of flower sellers and a fish stall remained. He bought a cheap throw away phone with a sim card in the first shop and did the same in the next four shops. This gave him five phones, enough for what he had in mind, lucky Mark Barry's shop was doing well, that was the only place he could get the money to buy what was needed.

Walking into the hotel, he found Stan already there sitting over a coffee. He had some scrapes and bruises and a plaster on his forehead.

"Stan, how are you?" Jack asked.

"I am fine on the outside," Stan replied, "but on the inside, I am dead. My little sister… Jack, I cannot get the picture of her dead body lying in my arms out of my mind. I keep thinking about the guy that I should have gone into the club after."

Jack took out the photographs and laid them out on the table. Straight away, Stan picked out the black curly haired guy with the X across him.

"That's him, Jack," Stan said with venom, stabbing the photo with his finger. "I know a bit about you and I have heard stories of your past life and the fact that you have these photographs means to me that you have something in your mind to deal with these madmen. I am a veteran from an elite force within the Croatian army. I fought for four years for my country's freedom from the Serbs. During that time, I did things that no man should have to do, but here, now, I will do whatever is needed and help you with whatever you have in mind. You see Jack, I, like you, must have revenge for what has been done."

Jack looked long and hard at Stan. He could sense that Stan was the real deal.

"Okay, Stan, you're in," Jack said and proceeded to bring him up to date on where they were at. He made arrangements to meet up that evening to go with him to pick-up the Doctor and find out where the remaining members of the group of bombers lived.

"Thank you, Jack," Stan said. "I will now go and prepare for what lies ahead. What is your situation regarding arms for the fight that is coming?"

"I have nothing at the moment, but we should be well covered within a week or so," Jack answered.

"Maybe I can be of help with the weapons that I have, which are a nine mil browning semi-automatic with three magazines with a total of 36 rounds and a sawn off shot gun with an amble supply of cartridges."

Jack was clearly impressed, as he laughed and shook his head.

"Fair play to you Stan, but there will be no need to bring them with you tonight," he said, as he gave him one of the phones. "Only use this to ring me on this number," he said, as he wrote down the number that he was going to use. "Call nobody else on it and give your information in less than a minute," Jack instructed as he handed over the slip of paper with his number on, "and keep it charged up at all time with plenty of credit on it."

Stan stood up and offered his hand to shake.

"I want to thank you for the chance to avenge my family's hurt, Jack. See you this evening," Stan stated before turning to leave the hotel.

Jack ordered a coffee while he waited for Tom Duffy.

At eleven o'clock on the dot, the slightly hunched figure of Tom Duffy entered the hotel. He walked on past the reception desk and the door leading into the bar and entered the small residents lounge. From where Jack was sitting, he could see Tom approaching.

"You didn't look into the bar for me, Tom?" Jack asked.

"Sure you told me that you are off the drink," Tom replied matter-of-factly, as he took a seat with his back to the door.

A young foreign-looking girl in a hotel uniform approached the table and they ordered tea and toast.

Jack's attention was drawn to a middle-aged suited man that he caught a glimpse of walking into the hotel seconds after Tom. The man's eyes searched the reception area and he then walked into the bar. Within seconds he walked back out into the resident's lounge, a startled look came over his face for a split second when he saw Tom sitting at the table with him, and he all too quickly turned and walked out again.

Jack watched him look around the reception area for somewhere to sit and then over his shoulder. There was nowhere that he could position himself without Jack being able to see him, so he walked smartly out of the hotel. Tom caught Jack's look.

"Is everything ok?" he asked.

"I think that we may have an uninvited visitor," Jack replied.

"Don't be silly," Tom said, "who in the world would know that me and you would be sitting here having tea and toast?"

"You're probably right," Jack said to appease Tom, as the tray with the tea and toast was placed on the table.

"Well, Jack," Tom said, "there seems to be a right bit of skulduggery going on; with brick walls cropping up all around this. There are a number of things bothering me; the first is that the man I brought the story and tapes to is an Assistant Commissioner," Tom said as he began to tell Jack all that had happened there, but decided to leave out the names of those in Garda HQ who vowed to help them. Tom thought that such sensitive information should be on a need-to-know basis.

Jack sipped his tea and ate his toast while listening intently to Tom. "Let me get this straight Tom," he said, wiping a few crumbs from his mouth, "are you telling me that there is something much bigger going on than lunatics blowing up people and being let get away with it? And that I may have been given a free run to sort them out but that I will be crucified if it goes wrong?"

There was a moment silence as Jack stared in disbelief at Tom.

"In a way, yes," Tom answered, "but I have a good man who will work with me to clear some of the way."

"It's the rest of the way that I am thinking about," Jack retorted.

"It's up to you, Jack," Tom said. "You are the one who came to me with the story and you seemed to be determined to get it sorted. And let's not forget that people are getting killed all over the place and it certainly looks like someone at the top of the so-called feckin' Establishment has a vested interest in stopping anyone interfering. Now you can walk away if you want, Jack, and I'll thank you for what you started."

Tom paused and leaned across the table. "But Jack, I don't think that you can do that," he added.

Jack said nothing for a couple of moments, just looked into his now-empty tea cup. Finally breaking the silence, Jack said, "Here," as he handed over the large envelope of photos, "these are still shots taken from the CCTV tape in the Internet café."

Jack pointed out the two with the X's mark. "These are the two from the LUAS bombs."

"And the third one with the X?" Tom asked.

"That's the one from the nightclub," Jack replied.

"How the hell did you get that?" Tom enquired.

Jack tapped his nose and winked at him.

"No, I need not ask," Tom added.

"The rest are still out there, Tom – and they all attend a small Mosque in Phibsboro. Can you see if they are on file anywhere? I need their addresses – and the quicker the better."

"I know where all this is going, Jack… and I believe that what you have in mind is the only way. I never thought that in my life I would be saying that to an IRA man! Do you need anything else along with the addresses?" Tom asked.

"No, but I have something else for you," Jack said, handing over one of the new phones to Tom, "only use this to call me and keep the call short and sweet, and also make sure that it is charged at all times, turned on and with credit in it."

Tom nodded his head.

"Here's my number to ring me," Jack added, as he wrote down the number on the hotel napkin.

"That's good thinking, Jack," Tom said, as he rose from the table, "little wonder that you gave us the run around."

Jack smiled.

Tom concluded, "I'm off now to meet a man that can help us. I'll ring you shortly with some word, I hope."

As Tom left, Jack got up and quickly walked over to the front window of the hotel reception area and looked out from behind the curtain. He could see Tom making his way through the crowd towards O'Connell Street – and there it was, what he had been hoping had not been happening: Tom was been followed. The guy in the suit that he'd seen earlier in the hotel, stepped off the LUAS platform where he had been loitering, pretending to be just another passenger waiting to get on the tram. He walked briskly after Tom and disappeared into the crowds.

Having been to the hotel many times over the years, Jack left by the back door, which led into a laneway that split three ways. Within seconds he was gone.

CHAPTER 13

After leaving Jack, Tom made his way slowly up Grafton Street, through the bustling throng of tourists, street artists and shoppers. He stopped for a few seconds at the flower sellers' stall, near the statue of the legendry musician Phil Lynott, marvelling at the sea of colours. As he made to move on, Tom suddenly got a strange feeling over him which caused him several times to check behind him. *'Eyes are definitely on me. Jack wasn't being paranoid,'* he thought. He then double backed towards Bewley's and instead of going in, he took the next turn on the left down a small side street. He stopped suddenly at the corner of another left, which led into an alley way and bend down to tie his shoe lace. *'Got you,'* he thought, as a clean cut, middle-aged man in a suit abruptly stopped and turned to look into a woman's underwear shop window.

Tom took his time and could see that the man was uncomfortable where he was standing and he was forced to walk into the shop. With that, Tom was up and dashed down the alleyway and into Bewley's café through the back door. He paused just inside the doorway for a moment or two to take a breather, and when nobody came in after him, he went in search of David, the Garda Commissioner's aide who was seated in a booth that faced the front door. David got a start when Tom quickly plonked himself down beside him.

"Did you not know that there is a small back door that you can come and go through?" Tom asked a momentarily flustered David, with a smile.

"You got me there, sir," David acknowledged

"Ah, you'll have to stop calling me sir; Tom is my name," he said. "Have you got anyone tailing me?"

"No, why?" David replied.

"Well someone has been following me. I've just lost him in the back street," Tom explained.

David glanced around, pale with worry.

"Here, I have something for you," Tom continued, taking out the envelope with the photographs. "These are close-ups of the tape in the Internet café of those feckin' madmen doing the bombings. Three of them have X's across them you'll notice; two are the LUAS bombers and the other is from the nightclub."

David looked through the photos.

"Snap," he said, handing Tom a file cover, inside were single page files with small photographs of young Muslim men attached to the corners of each page, Special Branch was stamped on each page with footnotes. Tom noticed that the notes pointed out that they were all members of the Mosque in Phibsborough. Tom also noted that the same house address was on the pages of some of the men and he compared them to the photos that Jack had given him.

"These are our men," Tom said, pointing out to David the faces, as he wrote down the house address.

"I agree with you there, Tom," David said, as he placed the envelopes that Tom had given him into his briefcase.

"Tom, this tail that you reckon you had coming here has me more than a bit perturbed," David said, glancing around again.

"Me too. I was half-hoping that it was you keeping an eye on me," Tom said.

"I'll have to look into it," David said, "is there anything else I can do for you?"

"Not at the moment, although I think that things are going to get a bit lively very soon from our side," Tom said. "So, I'll stay in touch."

Both men stood up shook hands and went their separate ways.

CHAPTER 14

With time to kill before the meeting with Donegal Phil, Jack took a leisurely stroll towards Mark Barry's shop. He had a double reason for going there, as he firstly wanted to check if he was being followed, as catching that tail on Tom had him thinking. He spent an hour walking through department stores; there was a bookies shop that he knew of where you could enter on Abbey Street and exit onto Sackville Row which he walked through, pretending to look at the form sheets of the day's races. Then there was a battered old pub that he knew where someone who was a little bit well-dressed would stand out a mile, but at the end of his experiment, he felt that he was clear.

He entered Barry's shop, which had a couple of customers being served in.

"Ah! There you are, sir," Mark called out, pretending that Jack was merely another customer, "your television is in the back repaired and ready for you. If you can just give me a few minutes to serve these customers, I'll be with you then."

"No problem, you carry on, I'm in no rush," Jack said. He spent the next ten minutes looking at all the electronic devices in Barry's shop. There were radio scanners of different sizes, microphones - big and small, anti-surveillance devices of all sorts. He smiled as he heard the last customer giving out about the price of his radio repair. When the shop emptied, Mark locked the door.

"Did you hear that fuckin' eejit giving out about the cost of repairing that fuckin' radio? It was for the scrapheap when he brought it in here and I felt sorry for him and I repaired it for him. Sure, I didn't charge him for half the stuff that I put into it," Mark complained.

"You're a big softy, Mark," Jack said, laughing.

"How are we getting on, Jack?" Mark asked.

"We're closing in, Mark. But something is bothering me. I met with Tom Duffy this morning and he was being followed, I know that he was and I can't figure out who they are and why they are following him. At the moment, I know that I am clear, but I have to assume the worst from here on."

Jack explained, "Do you have anything small, Mark, that could tell me if there was a directional mike pointing at me or if there was a bug nearby, you know what I mean?" Jack said.

"I know what you are looking for," replied Mark, "let me have a look on the computer – that will tell me what is in the shop."

After a few minutes searching the stock sheet on the screen, Mark said, "Bingo, I just might have something that should do the job."

He went into the back stores and returned with a small blue box thing that had a small red light on top.

"When you turn the switch at the side to on, this should tell you if anyone around you within a 100 metres radius is using an electronic receiving device," Mark explained. "Here, let me turn on a scanner at the end of the shop and you go to the door and turn that on. Now Jack, I have nothing turned on, so switch on the box."

"I've done that and nothing is happening," Jack said, but as soon as Mark turned on the portable scanner, the blue box lit up.

"There you are, Mark, it's on," Jack said, enthusiastically.

"So now, all you have to do when you go to meet someone is switch the box on; if there is anyone that is interested in your conversation and is using a receiver or a mike, you will know," Mark explained.

"Jaysus! If only we had some of this stuff back in the day, we certainly would have saved some people from getting killed or going to jail," Jack said.

"You're telling me. Now, take that with you," Mark said. "Is there anything else that I can do for ya?"

"Can you get your hands on a van by any chance?" Jack asked. "I think that we will be needing it within the next few days."

Jack's phone beeped; Tom had sent him a text message with the address of the bombers on it and he also confirmed that he had a tail.

"I knew I was right about Tom Duffy being followed, Mark. He has just text me to tell me so," Jack said.

"You are into very serious waters there, Jack," Mark said. "It could only be someone very high up that could sanction such a thing, or… what about an outside agency?!"

"Mark! You're dead right – that could very well be it," Jack said, excitedly, as he headed for the door.

"I'll have that van on standby from tomorrow on, just call into here when you are ready," Mark shouted after Jack, as he left the store.

"That's great, I have to go now to meet Donegal Phil," Jack said.

"Tell that madman that I was asking for him," Mark shouted after Jack.

"I certainly will," Jack replied, as he walked out the door.

Jack marvelled at the type of equipment that existed for surveillance, as he made his way to meet up with Donegal Phil. He was sure that the stuff Mark had in his shop was only the tip of the pile when it came to what Governments around the world had at their disposal. He recalled, as he walked, an incident at a training camp in the early morning, deep in the desert in Libya when the local people pointed out to him a small model airplane high in the sky and they immediately came under sustained fire. The first thing one of the locals did was shoot down the model airplane and they found that it had been carrying a camera which was able to direct the forces looking for them to their exact place; then they fought their way out of there. A shudder went through him at the memory of that close call – one of the many throughout his life, he recalled.

As he approached the pub that was the meeting place for Donegal Phil, he did a security check around himself as best he could and then entered through a side door.

Donegal Phil was a legend amongst Republican activists during the Struggles. Both he and Jack had taken part in many of the successful operations against the British forces, both in Ireland and abroad. His tactical ability to work out the finest detail in planning of operations was second-to-none and he was constantly called to Army Council meetings, where his opinion was valued. Things began to change for Phil after a number of new IRA members – all untried in war – began appearing at the council meetings; his opinion was less asked for and he resigned from active involvement because he had predicted the sell-out.

Phil was given a small run down cottage from an old friend in the middle of the Donegal mountains; it was miles from anywhere, which suited him down to the ground. As Phil was slowly renovating the cottage, he found that he had a knack for sculpturing with wood, so he began, as a hobby, making different shapes out of lumps of wood. Over time these sculptures were seen by others and were then sold for good money; his work became very sought after and so for years he enjoyed his life of solitude. Then one day, completely out of the blue, he got a message from Mark Barry that Jack had a problem and he knew that he had to go – he would never leave the mountain for anyone other than Jack.

Phil was sitting in the far corner with a coffee in front of him from where he could observe all that was coming and going and with the television placed over the door and horse racing on, to anyone interested, that was what he was watching. Phil was scrawny in appearance with long grey hair tied back in a ponytail. His face was thin and tanned from the sea breeze that blew up the Donegal mountains. He wore a plain black long sleeved t-shirt and torn blue jeans, which were not a fashion statement, but just his jeans; and while his boots were top of the range mountain walking boots, they had never seen a bit of polish from the day they were bought and lying across the haversack was a padded wind breaker jacket. His sinewy wrinkled fingers were rolling a cigarette with ease.

He never acknowledged Jack's entrance until he sat down beside him.

"Good to see you, Mo Sean Chara" he said, as they both embraced.

"Good to see you too, Phil," Jack replied.

"How is the boy getting on?" Phil asked. "Mark filled me in on some of the stuff that's happened."

"Coming on great. In fact, he's been discharged in a couple of days," Jack told him.

"A lucky young man," Phil stated, "and his mother?"

"Health-wise, she is fine, but things went really bad there between us," Jack replied. "All my fault… I went off the rails for a few years."

"I know, there were many times that I was going to come down from the mountain and kick the shite out of you from all the things that I'd been hearing," Phil said, as he took out his mobile phone and dismantled it.

"Good man, Phil, always the careful one," Jack said, as he ordered an orange juice. He then took out the little blue box and turned it on. "This is a small electronic sweeping devoice that I picked up off Mark, who by the way sends his regards, and what it does is alert me to any directional mikes or bugging devices that may be in the vicinity," Jack explained.

"I read about these things in a magazine," Phil said in amazement, "and these are the business, as they say now. Tell me all of what's happening and what we are going to do about it?"

Jack knew that Phil was a stickler for detail, so he slowly began to tell him where he was at, from the start up to the very minute they were at now, in between answering the many side questions that Phil had. Phil was curious about Stan and thought he could help them, but he was equally sceptical about the Muslim doctor and also with getting Tom Duffy involved, but Jack reassured him. The next hour was spent talking away in low voices and getting stern looks from the barman because they were not spending any money.

"Come on, Phil, you'll be staying with me for tonight, and you can decide in the morning if you want to be involved," Jack said. "I have to go and meet Stan and the Doc, so I'll leave you at my place. I know that you will go over all that we have spoken about so we can talk later."

"That'll do me; I'm knackered from the bus journey anyway," Phil said, as he put his phone back together and swung his knapsack over his shoulder.

Stepping outside the pub, a LUAS tram was standing at the platform and they hopped on board. Phil thought that this was a great thing.

"One of the many good things from the well-off years when everyone had a few euros," Jack remarked.

Within less than ten minutes, they were off the LUAS and entering Jack's flat; he was glad that he had cleaned up the place.

"Nice little spot you have here, Jack," Phil said.

"Thanks for being kind, but it needs a lot of spring cleaning."

"Ah, it's a real bachelor pad," he said half-enviously, making Jack feel that Phil was obviously living somewhere even more downmarket than himself.

"Our old friend, the Councillor, got me fixed up with it. Make yourself at home, I've to go out now and we'll talk further with the latest information when I get back. Do you want me to bring something back to eat?" Jack asked.

"No, you are alright, I'll look through the presses and the fridge and rustle something up," Phil said.

"Then you'll starve," Jack laughed. "I'll bring us back a curry, see you later."

Jack skipped out the door. As he sat into the car, Jack noticed a piece of paper stuck under the windscreen wipers, a parking ticket. "Fuck! I forgot all about those things," he muttered to himself, "that's Mark getting a little surprise in a few weeks."

He set off to pick up Stan and there he was, bang on time, standing, waiting like an animal ready to pounce. There was no conversation between them as they carried on to pick up the Doctor. He noticed Stan stiffen up as he pulled in to the pavement at the church in Phibsboro and the Doctor was standing there in his full Muslim regalia. Jack stopped the car alongside him. The Doctor threw a look around him and then he got in the back of the car.

"What the fuck is going on here, Jack?" Stan demanded. "Why are we dealing with this guy? He is one of them!"

"This is Doctor Kaleem; he is a friend of mine," Jack replied, angrily, "Doc, this is Stan – Stan lost his sister in the night club attack and nearly lost his own life that night."

"From my heart, I am truly sorry for your loss," the Doc said sorrowfully, as he stretched out his hand to shake. Stan did not acknowledge him. Jack made a mental note to sort that out later.

"Doc," Jack said, "I have confirmation on all that you told me about this group – and I also have an address. We will drop you off near the Mosque and head on to find this house. You can call me as they leave after prayer and we should be in a position to see them going home."

"That's sounds good," the Doctor said.

Jack then gave him one of the phones and instructed him as he did the others; he also wrote down his phone number and gave it to the Doc.

The Doc then directed Jack towards the Mosque.

"Jaysus! I never knew that this place existed," Jack said, as he watched people similarly dressed to the Doctor enter the red bricked two storey building. Jack then added, "Don't forget, Doc, short and exact on the phone and I'll catch you at the hospital in the morning."

Stan said nothing as the Doctor said goodbye. Jack looked at the piece of paper with the address on it and began to search for the street. After several minutes of getting nowhere, he spotted a guy in a uniform from a clamper van putting a clamp on a car and he drew up alongside.

"Excuse me there," Jack said, "can you tell me where this street is?"

The clamper guy looked at the slip of paper.

"That's only around the corner," he said, "go down the end of this road, take a right and then take the second left and there you are, but keep an eye out for the parking signs as only one side of that road is free parking."

"Thanks for your help and that parking tip," Jack said and drove off. He followed the instructions and within three minutes they were on the street. The houses were solid looking three storey ones with short gardens in the front. The street was lined with mature bushy trees. As they slowly drove down the street, Stan spotted the house number on a gate pillar.

"There it is, Jack," he said.

Jack noted that it was an end of terrace house with a narrow laneway at the side. The curtains were opened on the ground floor but drawn on the top two floors. The front door, Jack observed, was an old wooden one, not in the best of shape, unlike the doors on the other houses that were new looking PVC ones, so it hopefully meant that it didn't have a very strong lock on it either.

Jack parked up a bit past the house.

"I'll have to go back and check out that laneway, Stan. I'll leave the phone here with you and if the Doc rings, just tell him ok, I won't be long."

"Ok," replied Stan.

Jack left the car and scanned the area with his eyes as he walked. There were no CCTV cameras on the street and none on any of the houses, which was a good thing.

He slipped down the laneway and found an old wooden gate that opened into the back of the house. Lifting the small metal latch, the gate screeched open and he stepped into the rear of the house. There was a long overgrown garden, but most important of all there was no dog or cameras. Jack stood for a second, formulating a rough plan and when he was satisfied in his mind, he returned to the car.

"Your man rang two minutes ago," Stan said.

"Good," replied Jack, as he drove away and turned the car at the end of the street to enable them to see anybody walking down it and to also gave them a clear view of the gateway to the house. For the next ten minutes as they waited, it gave Jack the opportunity to explain to Stan who the Doctor was, what he had done for his son and that more than likely he would have been on duty, saving lives the night of the club explosion.

Stan apologised to Jack and before anymore could be said they spotted a group of similarly dressed young men walking down the street talking and laughing as they entered the house.

"Look at those bastards," Stan said with anger. "Fuckin' laughing with not a care for what they are doing, or for the damage and hurt that they have brought upon so many people..."

"Stan, you are going to have to calm down, or you are no good to me for what lays ahead," Jack warned him.

"Yes, you are right, Jack, but it is very hard for me, but I will be in control from here on," Stan promised.

"Let's go, I've seen enough," Jack said and he drove away, but he took his time to study the best and quickest way for getting away from the house.

They drove across town and Jack stopped the car to let Stan out.

"Stan, I really meant what I said about controlling your anger. We will deal with these madmen shortly and you will have your revenge, so stay calm and focus on the job at hand. Can you have the weapons ready for two days' time? And will you get ten shot cartridges for the sawn off?" Jack asked.

Stan nodded his head.

"I will be in touch with you on the new phone with arrangements, see you then," Jack concluded.

As he watched Stan got out of the car and slam the door in anger, Jack hoped that he hadn't made a mistake taking him on board. He didn't want a loose cannon – someone that would not follow instructions and blow the mission – but his gut feeling told him that he hadn't.

CHAPTER 15

Jack picked up a chicken curry on his way home. Back at his flat, he found Phil stretched out on the sofa watching an animal survival program on the television when he got in.

"Grubs up," he said.

As Jack put the kettle on and divided the curry in two, neither of them spoke until they had finished the food and drank their tea.

"Now tell me, what have you got in mind?" Phil asked.

"These madmen have to be wiped out," Jack started, "going to the Gardaí is not an option for us, as we don't know who is involved within them and doing nothing is not an option – so we have to keep it simple. Their base of operation is known to us, that's where I was tonight and we have the weapons along with the manpower to finish them off."

"Talk to me again and tell me all the way from the very start to this minute where we are at now," Phil asked.

Jack was not surprised at this request as in all the years that he knew Phil and through everything that they had been involved in together, he strove for perfection and only by having every little detail could he work out the situation.

When Jack was finished, Phil spoke: "You probably have not been following events around the world, but there has been reports in many countries about the American CIA kidnapping people who they deem to be Muslim fanatics and flying them to America for interrogation. They'd been doing it from a base in Germany but the German people rose up and protested against it. The same happened in France. So, I can see why they would create a situation in a country where nobody would object to them carrying on what they are doing and with their easy access to Shannon airport, Ireland would be a prime candidate," he said, pausing as Jack digested all this information.

Phil continued, "So, as you said about Tom Duffy being followed – he's the one that brought your information to the top brass within the Gardaí and whoever he passed it on to has alerted someone that they may have a problem. You will now be a candidate for watching, especially now that you have both been spotted together so care must be taken at all times. It is my opinion that based on all that we know, the Americans are up to their tonsils in this. I cannot see it being official policy but maybe there's a rogue element within their establishment with a lot to lose if Shannon Airport is closed to them."

"You're saying that all this carnage is down to business and finance?" Jack said, in a shocked tone.

"Yes, I am," Phil said, "there are billions of dollars at stake here, Jack – and they don't give a fuck about anything or anybody but their dollar. Now, Jack, you've been to the base of these madmen, so what's your plan of operation?"

Jack explained, "Well, they kneel down for prayer at mid-day every day, the Doc tells me, so at that time, the day after tomorrow, we will storm the house while they are praying. Stan and I will go in the front door, the Doc and you in the side gate to cover the back of the house. All inside are to be killed."

Jack paused and looked at Phil as he digested the plan. He then continued, "I will go through the front door with the sawn off with ten shot cartridges for the spread in a closed room, which should take out all that are in there and with Stan behind me using the handgun to finish off anyone that survives the initial onslaught. The Doc and you will be in the back garden with you carrying a handgun, if anyone comes out that way, you deal with them. We should be in and out within three minutes and away into the city streets."

"How are we getting there?" Phil asked.

"Mark Barry is fixing me up with a van that will suit our purpose tomorrow," Jack replied.

"Well, we know that Tom Duffy had a tail, so how do we know that the lunatics are not under observation?" Phil asked.

"They could well be and we will assume that they are, but my scanner showed no electronic activity going on in the area tonight – and if they do have someone in a house watching them, well by my reckoning, by the time they react and get back up there, we'll be well away from it," Jack answered.

Phil thought for a few moments, dissecting the plan in his head.

"I like it, Jack, plain and simple, in and out," he said.

"And now you have the sofa," Jack said throwing him a blanket, "I've the bed, see you in the morning."

"Good night, mo chara," Phil said, as they both settled down, each knowing that the next couple of days would be crucial to everyone's well-being.

Jack arose from his bed the next morning to find Phil hunched over his laptop.

"What's happening, Phil?" Jack asked, as he walked past him into the kitchen. "I'll put the kettle on," he added, somewhat sarcastically.

"What's the address you have for those boyos?" Phil asked.

Jack's curiosity was up and he walked over to Phil and looked over his shoulder at the laptop screen.

"What's that Google map search thing?" he asked.

"Wait till you see this," Phil said excitedly, "give us that address again."

Jack called it out and Phil tapped it into the computer and pressed the search button and within a few seconds an overview of Phibsboro appeared. Jack could plainly see the football stadium that he knew was Dalymount Park and the big church that stood in the fork of the road. Phil zoomed into the street address that Jack had called out.

"My Jaysus!" Jack said in amazement, "would you look at that... there's the house on the screen. Amazing..."

Phil laughed.

"Look at this," Phil said and as Jack watched, he felt that he was actually on the street outside the house; he could see the length of the street and all the cars parked on it. Phil zoomed in on the door, which as Jack had said didn't look too strong. Phil then worked the pointer on the screen and zoomed backwards from the house so that they could see the road network around the area.

"Look here, Jack," he said, "if we take this turn here and then the first right, we'll be well away and swallowed up within the city centre traffic in no time."

"This thing saves us from doing a dry run. It's marvellous," Jack said, patting his old comrade on the back. "It certainly beats scribbling rough drawings of the area and having them in your pocket. I take it that you are in then?"

"Of course I'm in, did you think that I would let you tackle this all on your own?" Phil asked, somewhat rhetorically.

CHAPTER 16

Tom Duffy spent a restless night in bed, tossing and turning. He was bothered by the fact that someone had him under surveillance. *'It has to be that bastard O'Sullivan, the Assistant Commissioner,'* he thought. But who was behind him? That was the question that had to be answered.

In the morning, as he pottered around the kitchen preparing his porridge, there was a loud knock on his front door. "Who could that be at this hour in the morning?" he asked himself. He looked out the window and saw a large red car with two aerials on top. He could make out two smartly dressed men at the door who looked like Gardaí. *'Maybe David had sent them out to look after me,'* he initially thought.

He opened the door and the two men flashed their ID cards at him, a bit too quickly for his liking.

"Let me see those ID cards again?" he asked.

One of the two then began talking while the other stood uncomfortably to the side looking around.

"You look like you have a nice place out here, Mister Duffy, all on your own and we know that you have given good service to the force over the years," the talker said in a patronising voice, "but at the moment it seems that you are mixing with strange company and we just want to make sure that you are on the same page as us. We believe that you would be better suited looking after yourself, Tom, minding your own business – and we would like to leave here believing that you will do that," he said threateningly.

"I've asked you both for a look at your ID cards already. So, I'll ask you one more time, show me your ID cards," Tom demanded defiantly.

The talker took a step forward.

"Don't make things awkward for yourself old man," he snapped. At that moment the postman pulled up in his van.

"Howya, Tom," he called out.

"I have those couple of cabbages here ready for you," Tom replied, as the postman walked up the pathway.

The two men turned and left hurriedly without any further talk. Tom followed them to the gate and took a mental note of the car registration.

"Is everything alright, Tom?" the postman enquired.

"Fine now, I wasn't too sure of those two buckos and you came at just the right moment," Tom answered.

"So, there is no cabbages for me then?!" the postman laughed.

"Next time," replied Tom, as the postman left.

Tom went inside and had to sit down to gather his thoughts. "Those two were actually threatening me, the fucking nerve of them," he said to himself. He picked up his mobile phone and rang David's number. David answered straight away

"What's up Tom?" he asked, with real concern in his voice.

"I've just had two detectives here trying to put the frighteners on me. They pulled the auld flash the ID cards too quick for me to make out who they were trick, but I got the registration of the car they were in," Tom answered, giving the car registration to David.

"Can you come up to the city this afternoon to meet me?" David asked. "I should have something on this by then. I'll see you around two o'clock, where we met before."

"I'll see you then," Tom replied.

*

David went straight to his Boss's office and he outlined to him what had just happened to Tom. He also informed him of the tail he had leading him to their previous meeting. The Commissioner slammed his fist on the table.

"The cheek of that O'Sullivan. I'll have him for this," he said with anger, then he wrote down a name and phone number and instructed David to ring it straight away and arrange a meeting. "Tell him that it is a call from me and that you will be going in my place."

He then told David that the name was a good contact and that he had built up a good working relationship with him over the many years that he was stationed in the American Embassy.

"This guy is not one of the new crowd, so you can trust him. I first met him when I was stationed in the States," the Commissioner said. "If there is any involvement of any kind from the Yanks, that man will find out. And David, do your best to protect Tom Duffy at all times."

"Consider it done," David said, as he exited the office.

*

Tom rang Jack on his new phone and told him that he would be up in the city in the afternoon. They arranged to meet in the same place as before at four o'clock, short and sweet as agreed and then phones off.

Tom then thought of an old partner of his in Special Branch, Sean Doyle, who was still in the force working behind a desk. He knew that he had his phone number in an old book of his, and on finding it he rang him to arrange to meet up. Sean would know who those two boyos were, or if not, he could find out, Tom knew. Although he had asked David to find out about them, he felt that it would do no harm going his own route as well. Having made the arrangement for one o'clock in a pub that they used to frequent not too far from Garda Headquarters, Tom remarked to himself, "Three meetings in one day, I might as well be back full-time!" He smiled to himself as he put his coat on and walked to the village to catch the bus.

*

Sean Doyle was sitting in a booth at the back of the pub with a half filled pint glass of Guinness and the remnants of a ham and cheese sandwich in front of him, a layer of crumbs sitting down the front of his cardigan.

"Ah, Tom, there you are," he said, as he wiped the crumbs from his mouth and from his front. "Will you have a pint?" he asked.

"No, Sean, a bit early for me, but a cup of tea would be great," Tom said. "This place hasn't changed much, except for the crowd. I half expected it to be full of Gardaí, like the old days."

"Ah, sure there's a new breed of Guard out there today, most of them will spend their lunch going for runs or in the gym. Sure, you'll hear nothing of what goes on at street level if you don't put a bit of time in at the pub," Sean stated.

"True for you Sean," Tom said.

Sean got up to order a pot of tea for Tom. When he returned with it, Tom thanked him and asked, "How are you getting on, and the family?"

"I'm just filling in time Tom, another three months to go and then the boss at home has a list of things the length of the street for me to do," Sean said, dejectedly.

"Now, Sean, you've been long enough a part-time husband, make the most of it and enjoy yourselves, the pair of youse," Tom advised. "I wish that I had gotten the time with Bridget to do that."

"I understand. Listen, it's great seeing you, Tom. Now what's up?" Sean asked.

While not telling Sean the whole story, he told him of meeting with O'Sullivan and after that his sense of been followed and finally his two visitors.

"First of all, Tom, you could have picked someone better than O'Sullivan to go to – he's the biggest shite bag that I have ever come across in the Force. He has built a small army of lackeys within, that's what I call them, who jump to do his bidding even before he asks and if you have hit on anything that could affect him, well, then you've a big problem," Sean said.

Tom took a sip of his tea.

"You said that you got the registration of the car?" Sean asked.

"Yes, I have it here," Tom replied, reading it out along with the colour and make.

"I can quite easily find out who those two are and from the job I have behind a desk, I can redirect their roster that it will take them to the arsehole of Kerry for a couple of weeks," Sean said, gleefully in a boyish voice, slapping his hands together in excitement at the thought of messing them around. "Hehe… and if there is anything else that you think of that I can help you with, Tom, just ring me to meet and I will be here."

"I don't want to get you involved, Sean; this is very serious stuff and you have only a couple of months left to serve," Tom said. "If you can do anything with what I have given you, will be help enough for me. Thank you."

"Tom, I know that you have not told me even half of what is going on, but I know you and it is something very serious and important – so, as I have said, if you need me for whatever reason, call me," Sean ordered.

"You're a good man, Sean," Tom said, draining his cup of tea and getting up from the table. "I'll be in touch," he said as he went to leave the pub.

Tom spent the next half an hour walking around the side streets and shops around Grafton street before he entered Bewley's Café through the back door. David was sitting to the immediate left of the door and Tom missed him as he walked in; for a couple of seconds Tom stood and looked around him then he felt a tap on his shoulder.

"Got you there, Tom," David said, laughing.

A startled Tom looked around.

"I'll give you that, David. I must be losing it," Tom said.

"This is not a good turn of events," David began, as Tom took a seat, "I've spoken to the Commissioner and he is hopping mad at the thought that two members of his Force would be attempting to intimidate you. Now, I've been in touch with a contact that we have with the Americans and, based on all that I could tell him, he has an idea that something sinister is going on and he has assured me that he will have more information for me over the next couple of days."

"I'm told from my own sources that those two boyos are part of an inner circle that O'Sullivan has, which could be a bigger problem for the Commissioner, if he is organising his own Force within the Force," Tom said. "Now, listen for a bit David, I am meeting Jack Maguire later and I have the feeling that they are ready to do whatever it is that they have planned. I'll learn what that is later – but, if I am right, there will be carnage and the Gardaí will have to react, as is the law. So, you don't contact me over the next couple of days, that way you are clear of everything. I will contact you and we will meet at the hotel at the top of the street, we've met here in this cafe twice, so now we will move on," Tom finished.

"I understand what you are saying, Tom. I'll be on standby, so we will let it go at that… just make sure that you stay safe yourself," David said and left the café.

CHAPTER 17

Jack was reading the morning paper as he sat behind the door that opened into the residents' lounge in the hotel where he had met Tom before. By sitting in the position where he was, anyone entering the lounge had to walk all the way in to look around and this enabled Jack to observe them before they saw him, which is exactly what happened when Tom entered, he almost walked back out until Jack coughed.

"There you are," Tom remarked.

"Old habits," Jack replied, with a smile, "Well, how are things going for you?"

"I never thought in a million years that I would be sitting down opposite you having a conversation like this one," Tom began, but, before he could continue, Jack placed his little blue box on the table and turned on the switch on the side, the light came on. "What the hell…" Tom stopped talking when Jack raised his finger to his lips as a "be quiet" signal. There was no change in the colour of the light.

"A bug finder, which also lets us know if there is a directional mike on us," Jack explained. "We are clear on both fronts."

"Well, I've seen it all now," Tom said. He then began to tell Jack as much as he felt the ex-IRA man should know of the events and the visitors of the past day. He left out any mention of the Garda Commissioner or his aide.

"There is something really heavy going on, from what I am getting," Tom said. "There seems to be an American connection to all this, along with people within the highest level of the Government, but who and to what end, at the moment, I can't work out."

"Well, there should be a right uproar, Tom, within the next day or so. I'm not waiting any longer, but its best that you are not aware of any of the details. I will ring you straight away when it's done and have whoever you are trusting within the Force on standby to move… and move fast."

Tom looked into Jack's steely eyes and decided that he should ask no more questions, but he knew there was going to be a lot of blood split in the name of revenge.

There was silence for a moment or two.

"How is your son getting on?" Tom asked.

"He's getting on great; he's getting discharged from the hospital tomorrow afternoon and we are lucky he has no long term injuries and hopefully he is young enough to forget what he has been through," Jack answered.

"That's good, that's really good," Tom said.

Jack stood up and left his paper on the table.

"Have a read on the way home," he said, "I'll ring you tomorrow early afternoon, all going well, to arrange to meet up the following morning. It will be in the Buttery Café in Trinity College for a change of venue."

Jack walked quickly out the back door and disappeared through the laneways. Jack spent the rest of the afternoon buying essential gear for the next day; he bought four sets of disposable overalls, green in colour; a box of latex rubber gloves; and two Walkie Talkie radios, making sure that they came with batteries included. He then made his way up to the hospital for six o'clock to see his son and catch the Doctor.

Jack walked into the ward and was in shock when he found that his son's bed was empty. Fearing the worst scenario, the hairs were standing on the back of his neck and his heart was pounding fast as he frantically searched for the Staff nurse and asked her where his son was.

"Oh, he was there just a few minutes ago," she said and seeing the look of shock on Jack's face, she smiled warmly in an effort to calm him down. "Why not try the computer games room next to his ward? He was in there earlier playing with another boy."

Jack found Ciaran dug into a game with another lad, as if nothing had happened. He smiled and decided not to disturb him and as he turned around, he bumped into the boy's mother.

"He looks in great shape and comes home tomorrow, Jack," she said.

"Yeah, the doc told me the other day; that's great news, isn't it?" Jack said.

There was a slight awkward pause between them.

"Jack," she said, "I'm delighted that you have been coming up to see Ciaran and I know that he really enjoys your visits, so what do you say that we ignore that court order for a while and see how things go?"

"I'd be delighted with that, Ann, thank you," Jack smiled. "I'm just going to see the doc for a minute and, if it's alright, I'll see you both tomorrow."

"We'll see you then," she said with a smile.

As he walked away feeling great within himself, Jack heard her call after him.

"Jack I can sense that you are on to something, so be careful will yah?" she said.

Jack nodded his head towards her and walked away. He caught the Doctor in his office and told him the plan for the next day.

"Look, Doc, you're in the business of saving lives, not taking them, so I'll understand if you want to back out and leave this to us professionals."

"I am up for whatever we have to do. I will save more lives by helping you to kill these violent animals and ensure they don't kill again."

"That's a healthy way to look at it alright," Jack said.

Jack arranged to pick him up at 11.30 the next morning. As he was giving him his set of overalls and gloves, Jack noticed plastic overshoes on a table that were used in the operating theatre; so, he asked the

Doctor for four pairs, which he got. He then told the Doctor to have them with him to put on as soon as he got picked up next day. Jack then filled the Doctor in on his role and asked him if he had any questions.

"No, Jack, no questions. You know what you are about, I trust that," he said.

Jack then asked him if there was somewhere in the hospital that they could use as a 'run back to' safe house after they were finished.

The Doctor thought for a moment. "There is an ideal room, it's a wash room with showers, on the second floor off the car park. I will have the key and we can wait there for several hours," he said.

"Good man," Jack said, "that sounds ideal."

The next port of call for Jack was to Stan. Stan had got himself a two-bedroom apartment on the second floor of a complex in the Docklands, which looked out over the basin of the Grand Canal. This area had been a hub of activity over the centuries with the use of the canals to ship goods all around the country, but had fallen into a bad state of ruin for a number of years, only to be re-invented as a much sought after trendy place to reside in the property boom.

Stan had decorated the place really well, with small flower baskets out on the balcony, which were well cared for and had some great coloured flowers growing in them.

Jack was somewhat surprised at the near perfect condition of the apartment. As Stan was in the kitchen making coffee, Jack could see the many photographs of his family and, in particular, many of his deceased sister. He had built a small shrine in the centre of the sideboard around a large photograph of his sister adorned with rosary beads and candles. *'I didn't take him for a religious guy?'* Jack thought.

When Stan came back in with the coffees, Jack said: "Your sister was a very beautiful young woman."

Stan placed the coffee down on a small circular table in the middle of the room.

"Yes, she was," Stan said, sorrowfully, as he looked lovingly at the large photograph.

Jack took out his little blue box and turned it on; the light stayed its white colour.

"It's a bug and radio wave finder," Jack explained, yet again.

"I know; I have seen them in use before, many times, my friend," Stan said.

They both sat down and Jack then went over the plan for the next day; the same way that he had done with the Doctor.

"You will come in behind me Stan," he said. "I will have the sawn off shotgun... did you get the cartridges with the big shot inside?"

"I made them myself to suit our purpose," Stan replied.

"Good, very good. I intent to put them down before they can rise from their knees from prayer. Stan, your job in all this is to make sure that they are dead and to cover my back. The back entrance to the house will be covered and I want us in and out in two minutes. Stan," Jack asked looking straight into his eyes, "can you do what we need to do here?"

"Oh, yes, Jack," Stan said firmly, as he fixed his eyes yet again on his sister's photograph, "I can do what we have to do here."

Stan walked out of the room into the bedroom and returned with a leather holdall. He opened it up and took out the weapons, spreading them out on the floor: the sawn off and the two handguns. Jack could see that they were in pristine condition.

He handed Stan his overalls, gloves and overshoes and told him to be waiting at the bus stop outside his apartment block at eleven o'clock the next morning.

Stan stood up and thanked Jack again for the opportunity to avenge his sister and then let him out of the apartment.

Later that evening, Jack caught Mark locking up his shop.

"Mark, the van?" Jack asked. "How are we fixed?"

"Follow me," Mark said, leading Jack to the ground floor of the car park and showed him the van. It was parked in a corner behind a concrete pillar, hidden from camera view.

"Here you are," Mark said, throwing the keys over to Jack. "She has plenty of diesel in her and she is running well and I have also wiped her down thoroughly to clean any prints of mine off."

"That's great, Mark," Jack said. "I'll leave your car parked as near to the van as I can in the morning and I'll put the keys on top of the back wheel on the driver side for you."

"Do you need me for anything?" Mark asked.

"Not for this," Jack answered, "but we will need you after when we see what the fallout is."

"That will do; you know where I am," Mark said, "and good luck."

They shook hands and then they parted company. When Jack arrived home, he found that Phil had been busy both cooking and on the Internet. There was a pot of hot stew on the cooker. Phil poured out two big bowlfuls, along with two large glasses of milk and a couple of chunks of bread and butter.

"This is great stuff, Phil, haven't had a stew like this in years," Jack said in between spooning large amounts into him.

When they had finished, Jack cleaned up and they both sat down with a mug of tea in their hands. Jack then went through the day's meetings; firstly, Tom Duffy's; then the Doctors; and then Stan.

"It's interesting that Tom Duffy is thinking there's an American connection," Phil said, pointing to his laptop. "Here look at this – this is something I came across while browsing through it earlier."

He had found the name of the American company that was engaged in transporting the American soldiers through Shannon Airport and from that he found the names of the Directors of that company. All were ex-servicemen, except one – he had the same surname as the current American Ambassador and on delving further, Phil discovered that they were brothers.

"Isn't that a coincidence?" Phil asked.

"Coincidence me bollix," Jack said.

"And look at their financial losses last year, when the whole of the country was up in arms demonstrating and protesting about foreign troops on Irish soil," Phil added, "it definitely would be of no surprise to me if there was collusion of some type between this company, someone in a high place within the Government and the mad Muslims, with the strings being pulled by the Americans."

"Well then, with that being the case, we are certainly going to stir up a hornet's nest tomorrow," Jack remarked.

"Oh, that we will, my friend," Phil agreed, "that we will."

Jack and Phil were up and about early the next morning; they were both silent and a nervous tension could be felt in the flat as each man got himself mentally prepared for the day ahead. Phil put on the overalls over shorts and a t-shirt; he wore black runners and put both the latex gloves and the plastic overshoes in his pocket. They shared a mug of tea and a couple of pieces of toast.

"How are you feeling this morning?" Jack asked Phil.

"Ready," was all Phil replied.

Jack knew from their past activity that Phil would not be saying much, that he was now mentally prepared for the work ahead.

"Then let's go and do this," Jack said, as he took a black plastic bin liner bag from out of the press and stuffed it into his pocket.

They drove Mark's car to the IlAC shopping centre car park and found a spot beside where the van was parked. Jack looked around the place to make sure nobody was looking before putting the keys on the back wheel, as he had told Mark. He then slipped into his overalls. Then, both of them climbed into the van but not before putting on their gloves and their overshoes. They were now in operation mode. Jack started up the van and away they went.

The Doctor was waiting, ready, at the pickup point near the hospital. As the van pulled up, he put his overshoes and gloves on and then got in the side door into the back. Jack introduced Phil to him and they set off.

Stan was waiting at the bus stop with a new haversack slung over his shoulder. He had a pair of woollen gloves over his rubber ones and he put on his overshoes before stepping onto the open side door. Once in, he took off the woollen gloves and put them in the haversack.

"Everyone ok?" Jack asked.

They all nodded their heads and Jack swung the van out into the traffic towards Phibsboro. There was no talk, only the sound of the radio playing, but nobody was listening to that. Each of them were going over their own thoughts on what possible danger lay ahead. Twenty minutes later, they sat in the van a couple of doors up from the house off the old Cabra Road that they knew the suicide bombers were in. They knew that there were four of them inside. Jack turned on his little blue box and the light went red.

"We have some electronic activity around us," he warned them.

"The house is probably under surveillance," Phil suggested.

"We are going in anyway," Jack said, "remember, two minutes and back out, no delays."

He went over the plan again and told each man to check their weapons. He had the sawn off double barrelled shot gun with two cartridges with six pellets in each and he put four others into his pocket. Jack knew that the scatter of the shot would down several people straight away, giving Stan the time to move in and finish them off with the nine mil browning handgun. Phil and the Doctor both knew that they were to come in the back way. Phil checked his weapon, another nine mil browning with a full magazine of nine rounds. He put one round up the chamber and clicked the safety catch on. He knew the importance of making sure that nobody got out past them.

*

Further up the street, unseen by Jack, there was a large white van parked with blacked-out windows, which was part of the surveillance team that the American undersecretary from the Embassy had put in place. Inside, there were two agents sitting in the back who were wondering about the green Hi-ace van that had just parked on the street, but they dismissed it from their attention as they were closely studying a bank of television screens that showed all that was going on in the house and they paid no further attention to the Hi-ace. As all in the house got on their knees for prayer at noon, one of the agents in the van turned to pour out two coffees. At that very moment, the screens went mad with action.

"Would you look at this!" the watcher shouted, excitedly pointing at the screens, "what the fuck do we do here?"

The man collecting the coffee spilt the flask all over the place in his haste to turn and see what was going on.

"Goddam it!" he screamed, "I'm scolded," he cried in pain as the hot coffee fell onto his crotch, but he forgot about the pain when he saw what was happening on the monitors.

CHAPTER 18

Jack checked with everyone that they were good to go before the doors of the Hi-ace slid open. Within seconds, Jack was dashing up the pathway. He smashed through the door with his shoulder, quickly followed by Stan. Jack ran down the short hallway to the front parlour where three of the bombers were rising from their knees. Jack let both barrels of the sawn-off shotgun rip, hitting all three of them and amid their screams, Stan walked over and put a bullet in each of their heads. There was blood splattered everywhere. As their dead bodies fell backwards onto the ground, Jack was reloading and running up the stairs, as Phil and the Doctor burst in through the back door.

"We are missing one," Jack shouted, as he frantically ran from room to room.

After the sound of the smashing of the front door, the fourth bomber, who was upstairs, had grabbed his rucksack and leapt out the front window into the garden and was running away. Jack was going mad.

"Where's the little bollix?" he screamed out.

"I see him," Stan shouted, as he fired two shots through the glass of the front bottom window after him.

"Don't go into the street after him, Stan," Jack shouted, "all back to the van; it's time to get to fuck out of here."

As he ran back down the stairs, he noticed the Doctor cradling one of the bombers in his arm.

"What are you doing, Doc?"

"He spoke before he died, Jack," the Doctor said, "he asked for forgiveness and said something else."

"Never mind that for now, Doc – we have to get the fuck out of here," Jack shouted at him.

They all dashed back out to the van. Jack turned the key and gunned it out of the street. He could hear the wail of police sirens in the distance.

"How the fuck did they get on to this so quickly?" he asked out loud.

*

The two Americans in the van looked at each other in shock. The scolded coffee collector pressed a button on his mobile phone that fed into a room in Garda headquarters, which in turn started an emergency response.

"Did we just witness the execution of those three people?" the watcher asked rhetorically, in a shocked voice, while looking transfixed at the screens. They had watched the guy jumping out of the top bedroom window with a rucksack, escaping, and did nothing about him. They watched the green van speed away and when they heard the sirens in the distance, they calmly turned off all screens and at a leisurely pace drove away from the scene.

*

Jack rang Tom Duffy as soon as they had turned off the street.

"Tom," he said, "you should get your people to that address you gave me, we have taken out three of them but one bird flew the nest with a rucksack full of explosives. I could hear the police sirens in the distance as we were leaving… how come they were on to it? Because we were only in there for no more than three minutes, Tom. There are only three bombs left in that house. The fourth one is out there now."

"Jesus, Mary and Joseph, Jack."

"I'll meet up with you in the morning where we said at ten o'clock," Jack finished, and turned the phone off.

Tom immediately rang David as arranged to tell him of the events and for him to get to the house first before, what he believed, was O'Sullivan's squad. They also agreed to meet the next day at twelve o'clock.

David scrambled an armed response unit of two cars, which were on patrol in the city centre area. He instructed them to detain anyone that they found at the house – Gardaí included, no matter what rank they held, until he got there. He left Garda Headquarters at great speed with a car full of trusted Garda. They got to the house in breakneck speed of eight minutes to find the two armed response units near to fisticuffs with a parked Special Branch car with two men inside, as David had ordered, nobody had been allowed leave the crime scene.

David's men took over and on his instructions searched the house and located the three bodies along with the rucksacks full of explosives. David made a point of going through the house and leaving the Special Branch men detained outside.

"Jesus… this is some blood bath," he remarked to one of his men. "Check the dead against the photographs to see that we have all of the suicide bomb suspects."

"We had better get the Bomb Squad here," one of his men suggested, "there are three rucksacks full of explosives wired and ready to go."

"Ok, let's clear the building," David ordered.

The man who was checking the photographs to the bodies came over to David.

"They are all on our list except this one who is missing," he said, pointing to a photograph.

"Ok then, get his photo out to all units and tell them to approach with great care – to shoot first before talking, if they feel that they have to," David said, before then walking out to the pavement where the two Special Branch men were being detained.

"Who gave you the shout to get here?" he asked one of them.

"We were just passing by!" he replied.

"Ah, a smart fucker," David said. "Put him under arrest and get him to HQ."

The Sergeant in charge of the armed response unit took out his handcuffs.

"You can't do this," the Branch man cried.

"Take it up with the Commissioner next time you see him," David replied, turning to the next Branch man.

"Go fuck yourself," he said to David. David nodded to the Sergeant, "Him as well."

The two were put into a car kicking and cursing all sorts of stuff until a few well-placed digs from the Armed Response boys quietened them down. Nobody, it seemed, liked Special Branch men.

Before he drove off, the Sergeant asked where the third guy who was in the Special Branch car was gone. David spun round.

"What third guy?" he asked.

"There was a well suntanned guy, around six-foot-tall, tight blonde hair cut, looked like a Yank but said nothing and with all the commotion that was going on, he must have slipped away," the Sergeant explained.

"They'll tell us," David said, as he motioned for them to drive off.

The Bomb Squad then appeared and David briefed them on what the situation was, he advised them to check the whole house from top to bottom for anything else. It wasn't too long before a cavalcade of news reporting vans with their satellite dishes on top arrived on the scene. The reporters began firing questions at the person they deemed to be in charge.

"What's the read? We hear that this is a bomb factory for the suicide bombers who have been active in the city?" one reporter asked.

"We are evaluating the situation. At the moment this is a crime scene. A full statement will be issued in due course," David responded, wondering how the media were so quick to get to the scene and how they got the bomb factory slant on what was happening.

An Army ambulance parked up alongside the Bomb Disposal lorry and began to take the three bodies away, as each one was being cleared of any hidden surprises by the Bomb Disposal unit.

"What has really happened here?" the reporter asked again, whilst looking at the bodies that were being carried out on the stretchers, when suddenly a strong guise of wind blew the sheets off one of the bodies.

"Hey! These are Muslim men," he shouted, sniffing the story of his life.

"As I have already told you, a statement will be issued in due course," David repeated, as he ordered a car full of uniform Garda, which had arrived on the scene, to clear the area.

CHAPTER 19

After Jack made the phone call to Tom Duffy, he settled down to carefully driving the van across town – no speeding, indicating and slowing down wherever he had to. He was taking deep breaths to slow his body down and his mind was carefully going over all the details of the operation that they had just carried out. It was while he was going back over in his mind when he first drove into the street that the large white van with the blacked-out windows came to him, then the radio wave finder's activity. There was no doubt that the house was under surveillance by someone and they had done nothing to stop them, or the fourth bomber who got away, and that was going to be a serious problem. It was a good thing for them that he had anticipated such a thing going on, hence the two-minute time frame for going in and getting out.

One Bomber getting away was bad, he knew.

The Hospital entrance came into view and Jack calmly followed the signs to the car park. He called to the Doctor to come up front and guide him to the spot in the car park that he had in mind. The Doctor directed Jack to park at the perfect spot beside a doorway. Unseen by any camera or person, in a corner filled with large rubbish bins, they quickly exited the van and followed the Doctor through the open door. This led them down a short passageway to another door, which the Doctor then unlocked.

"Right, lads, strip off, overalls, shoe covers and gloves in here," Jack said, as he held open the black plastic bin liner that he had brought along.

After this, Jack ordered, "Showers for everyone," as he pointing to the shower cubicles in the corner of the room. "And rinse your hair and under your nails thoroughly," he added.

Stan gathered up the weapons and wiped them down, then packed them away in his rucksack.

When all was done, the four of them sat down on the floor with their backs resting against the wall.

"Well, we missed one of them," Jack began.

"That is my fault," Stan said, "I had him in my sights but a movement from one of those on the ground distracted me for a second."

"There is nothing that we can do about that now," Phil said. "It's what do we do from here?"

"We have to try and work out what we think the next target is going to be," Jack said.

"The one who spoke to me before he died," the Doctor began, "it was very hard to work out what exactly he was saying, he was asking for forgiveness and said what I took to be Corky Park, something like that.

"Corky Park! What the fuck is that?" Jack asked. Then after a few seconds he remembered, "There is a Corky Park in Clondalkin, off the Naas Road. It's a large public park with playgrounds for children, with an animal farm and picnic areas... lots of families make use of its facilities, but nothing that I can think of where large amounts of people gather, which, to date, has been their type of targets."

"Can we check if there any events – carnivals, concerts or the likes in that park this weekend?" Phil asked.

They spent the next couple of hours discussing all possibilities between them.

"It's time to separate and go," Jack said, "just wait till I dump this bag of clothes and get back."

Jack walked back out to the car park, careful to avoid any cameras and went to one of the large rubbish dumpsters where he threw the bag in and covered it up with some of the rubbish that was already there.

On his way back, he could not help but notice the amount of small flags attached to the windows of cars: Dublin colours and Donegal colours. Then he stopped in his tracks for a second. "That's it," he said out loud, "Croke Park, not Corky Park. The All-Ireland Football Final... it's on this weekend."

He ran back to the room.

"I have it," he said excitedly, as he re-entered the room. "It's the All Ireland Football Final in Croke Park, not Corky Park."

There was stunned silence as each man digested Jacks words. Stan and the Doctor looked at each other for guidance Croke Park meant nothing to them.

"Of course," Phil explained, "the biggest football match on the calendar. Everyone in the Government will be there. The cameras broadcast the match worldwide to millions of people, so it's ideal for someone who wants to make a point or statement to the world."

"Corky Park, Croke Park," the Doc said, "that could very well be it."

"Listen," Jack said, "this is Thursday and I meet with my contact tomorrow morning at ten o'clock. Phil, both you and the Doc make your way to Stan's place for twelve o'clock. Stan will meet you both at the bus stop where we picked him up this morning. Everyone think on the scenario that is emerging and what we can do about it and we'll talk further on it then."

Stan nodded his head.

"Right then, all head off for now, in different directions," Jack ordered, as he held the door open for Stan to go first; he was followed a minute later by Phil. The Doctor led Jack through the hospital to his son's ward.

When Jack reached the ward where his son had been, he again saw that the bed was empty but this time there were no sheets, blankets of pillows – all were gone, he looked into the computer games room and it was empty. He then approached the nurses station and asked a nurse them where his son was.

"Oh, he was discharged just over an hour ago, both he and his Mother seemed to wait around for a while and then they left," the Nurse informed him.

'Fuck! Fuck! Fuck!' Jack inwardly screamed at himself, *'another mess.'*

He walked out through the reception area of the hospital into the crowd of people that were coming and going. He passed a news stand and noticed the headlines on the front page of the early evening newspaper: SLAUGHTER IN PHIBSBORO it screamed in banner headlines. He bought the paper and read the fabricated story, which outlined how an armed response unit of the Garda, acting on information received, raided a house off the Old Cabra Road, where, after a brief gun battle, three men – believed to be part of the suicide bomber group operating in the city – were shot dead. A large amount of explosives were discovered in the follow-up house search. The article went on to praise the work of the Garda and said how the people of Dublin could now rest easy.

"What a load of shite," Jack thought, but he could see the logic of the Garda taking the credit for the raid and how it covered his boys and all that had happened. But to say that the people of Dublin could rest easy, that only made it easier was for the bomber who got away and was obviously plotting what could potentially be the biggest ever terrorist attack on the island by hitting Croke Park.

He brought the paper home and gave it to Phil to read. Phil was of the same opinion as Jack on the article about the Garda doing a good job on covering them.

"Is the boy alright?" Phil asked.

"I was too late as always. He had gone home with his mother by the time I got there," Jack sighed.

"I know that it's hard, Jack, but we have a job to finish and then you can sort out whatever has to be sorted," Phil stated.

Jack looked at Phil for a couple of seconds.

"You're right, Phil," he said. "Let's talk about this All-Ireland Football Final and the layout of Croke Park."

"I'll get it up on Google Map on the laptop and we can work out the placing of where everything is. I haven't been in the new Croke Park," Phil said.

"Great idea, Phil. I haven't been there either since I stood on the Hill in the old days," Jack reminisced. "You would not believe the amount of Republican activist's meetings we had using the cover of matches on that Hill."

They spent the next few hours going over the stadium. From the entrances used by the crowd, to the way into the dressing rooms under the stands that the team buses used, they could see the corporate boxes that circled three quarters round the stadium and the stairways to the upper stand. Then they tried to get into the mind of the bomber – where would he strike? If killing numbers was the aim, then the Hill – the only unseated area were the fans stood in large numbers together – was the spot, but then the President's box would have an International impact, with the eyes of the world looking on. They looked at the stadium structure to see if there was a spot that, if it was hit, would bring the upper stand down, which would affect several thousand fans.

And then Phil voiced the idea that the whole world, millions of people, would be watching their television sets when the Artane Boys band played the national anthem. The boy band were world famous thanks to having Larry Mullen of U2 fame as a former member and once being on the cover of an INXS album.

"For effect, that would be a time to strike," Phil observed.

They both decided to retire to bed with their heads full of the ifs and buts and maybes of the situation.

"We'll talk further in the morning," Jack suggested.

CHAPTER 20

The next morning, Phil was awake and up first. He turned on the television for the early morning news. He froze at what he saw on the screen.

"Jack! Jack! Get out here quick," he called out.

Jack jumped up out of the bed, thinking that they were being raided.

"What's up?" he asked, wiping the sleep out of his eyes.

Phil just pointed at the television. There was a live broadcast from Dublin Airport of a bomb explosion with multiple casualties, dead and injured. Jack stood in a state of shock, holding onto the back of the sofa to keep his balance. Nothing was said for what seemed like hours as they watched the carnage unfold live on the screen. Eventually, Jack shook himself awake.

"Did we call it wrong, Phil?" he asked. Phil walked over to the kitchen, filled the electric kettle with water from the tap and turned it on.

"I don't believe that we did. I've spent most of the night going over what has happened and the way these guys have been operating. They started off by announcing themselves with the two attacks on the LUAS, hitting ordinary people going about their everyday activity. Then, they hit the nightclub aiming at the young people who would not have thought too long about the LUAS blasts, especially while out dancing. Then, we all but wiped out their campaign, which to me was always heading for a spectacular finish. As bad as this airport hit is, it's not the finale, in my mind," Phil concluded.

"Are you saying that this was on the cards all along... that the last man continued with the plan that they had?" Jack asked.

As Phil poured out the tea, he replied, "I am, Jack. These people will carry out their instructions to the letter – and the one that got away, if his instructions were to hit the airport, well, nothing was going to change his mind," Phil pointed out. "No, Jack, to me, the Croke Park job is the finale."

"There must be more suicide bombers," Jack mused out loud.

Later that day, as Jack walked through the city streets towards Trinity College and his meeting with Tom Duffy, he could see the fear in the people's faces; their eyes were scanning everywhere and on everybody, especially anybody with a rucksack on their back.

Walking under the archway into the university through the bustling crowd, Jack could hear no laughter, he could see nobody smile, but he could hear whispered conversation between small groups of students. The tension was palpable. The city was in a bad way.

Tom was sitting in a corner with a small pot of tea on the table in front of him. Jack sat to the side of the table to enable him to see who was coming and going. He turned on his little blue box for detecting radio waves: all was clear.

"Well," said Tom, "I suppose that's the end of it now… with the last man blown himself up at the airport and all those unfortunate people killed or maimed. It's an awful pity that he got away, otherwise you would have done the perfect job."

"Tom, I don't believe that it's over," Jack said with conviction. "I believe that they have one more job to do."

"Oh, you do, do you?" Tom said in amazement, shaking his head, "but the bombers are now all dead! You made sure of that…"

Jack went on to explain to him what the Doctor had heard the dying bomber say and that after they, as a group, had went over it again and again, they concluded on Croke Park.

"And besides where were the three bombs that were found in the house going?" Jack asked

"CROKE PARK!" Tom almost shouted, "Have you gone mad Jack Maguire? There is no way that anything like that – what you are suggesting – could happen there. No way at all. The security's too tight."

"It didn't stop them hitting the airport. I'm telling you now, Tom, that's where they are going to hit," Jack said emphatically.

Tom sat silent for a couple of minutes.

"Jack, you said at first that you thought that Corky Park was mentioned?" Tom asked.

"That's right," Jack answered

"Well, let me tell you this, in complete confidence," Tom paused, "nobody amongst the public is aware that the British Prime Minister is flying in to meet up with the Government the day after tomorrow, and that he is flying into Baldonnell Airfield."

"The military airport, so?

"Well, it's right beside the Corky Park that you mentioned, which runs alongside the Naas Road… that has to be it," Tom finished.

A thoughtful look came over Jack's face.

"There is one sure fire way that we can find out," he said, after a pause.

"What way is that?" Tom asked curiously.

"We could lift the mad Mullah tonight and I can assure you that we will have the information that is needed by tomorrow morning," Jack said.

Once again, Tom went silent for a number of minutes.

"I am going to meet my contact at twelve o'clock. He will fill me in on what they got in the house and I'll ask what he thinks of your idea. I'll ring you straight after," he said.

"Ok, I'll wait for that call, but Tom," Jack said, "there is no other way."

As he left the university's grounds, Jack thought, *'Wait for the call, me bollix.'*

He met up with Phil and the Doctor at Stan's apartment. The television was on broadcasting from the airport. The visual scenes were horrific. Jack walked over and turned the television off.

"Here is where we are at," he said and he went on to explain to them about Tom Duffy's theory that the British Prime Minister was the target. Phil asked for a bit of time to digest the new information while the Doctor was of the belief that the Airport had been the last job.

Stan turned to Jack.

"What do you think, Jack?" he asked.

"There are two scenarios on the table, as I see it – and we could spend forever trying to work our way through them… time that we don't have, but I believe that there is one man in this town that knows what is about to happen and I am of the opinion that we lift him tonight and get all the answers that we need," Jack said.

"Who is that man?" the Doctor asked.

"The mad Mullah himself," Jack answered.

Phil then came out of his thoughts: "You've hit it right on the nail, Jack."

"He could be taken from his house at the rear of the Mosque tonight, after prayers," the Doctor suggested. "I could make an appointment to meet with him when everyone has gone. The only one who

159

could possibly be around at that time would be his driver, who also acts as the caretaker. And that room at the hospital car park, which we used, would still be free if we were to bring him back there in complete privacy."

"We could keep him at the Mosque, in his living quarters?" Jack stated.

"We could indeed, Jack," replied the Doctor, "his house is a small single storey building that sits on its own behind the Mosque, out of view from the road."

"Well, that's the place then," said Jack, turning to Phil.

"It would save a lot of risk, like dragging him into a van with him screaming and shouting... plus we know that there is more than likely surveillance on the place," Phil pointed out.

"Right, so, Doc," Jack said, "you make the arrangements for the meeting. I'll go with you if you can get me appropriate clothing and when we have him, we'll ring Stan and Phil to come in with the van. What time suits?" Jack asked, turning to the Doctor.

"I would say that 10.30 would do us," the Doctor answered.

"I'll need a hand gun, Stan," Jack said.

"What about a stun gun?" Stan answered.

"That will do even better," Jack replied.

With that, Stan walked into his bedroom and returned with a stun gun.

"Jaysus, Stan, is there anything that you haven't got?" Jack asked, laughing.

"You've used one of these before, Jack?" Stan asked.

"No," Jack replied, "give me the rundown on it and I'll be fine."

Pointing to the two small brass needles sticking out of the top, Stan said, "You make sure that these two points are touching him and then you press this button on the side, and then an electric current flows through him and he is knocked unconscious."

Stan pressed the button and an electric spark flashed between the two points, which caused the Doctor to jump with fright. Jack then took the stun gun in his hand and repeated the action that Stan had just done.

"I have that now," said Jack "... okay then, let's say that Croke Park really is the target, have we thought out any plan of action?"

"An old army friend of mine from Croatia works there as a grounds man," Stan said. "I contacted him this morning in anticipation of us having to move and anything that we want him to do, he's on board."

"Have him check out all staff or contractors that may be working around the presentation podium from today onwards," Phil suggested.

"Phil," Jack said, "Albert Green, who we both knew well, as a fringe active Republican, runs the security for the stadium on match day. So, why not contact him today? And fill him in with as much as you think that he needs to know at this stage, because he can be trusted," Jack directed, as he searched through his mobile's contacts for Albert's phone number.

"That will be no problem," Phil said. "I'll meet him this afternoon".

"Right then, let's get moving," suggested Jack. "Stan and Phil will be ready for pickup at the corner of the Old Cabra Road near the Mosque, from ten o'clock on. I'll pick up the Doc at 9.45 at the hospital and then travel across town to you." They finished up and went their separate ways; Stan to his grounds man friend; the Doctor back to the hospital; and both Jack and Phil started back to the flat.

On the way, Phil rang Albert to arrange a meeting. Albert was completely stunned to hear Phil's voice as a shiver went up and down his spine.

"I need to see you urgently, Albert," Phil said with authority.

"I'm up to my eyes at the moment, getting things ready for this All-Ireland tomorrow," Albert whined.

"Perhaps you did not hear me, Albert, I need to see you straight away," Phil stated again.

"Alright, alright, but it will have to be around nine o'clock tonight at the hotel here beside Croke Park," Albert relented.

"That will be fine. See you then," Phil replied.

After he hung up the phone, Phil turned to Jack and said, "That fella's never changed, still whinging… Fuck! Jack, I forgot about ten o'clock tonight… lifting the Mullah!"

"It's important that you see Albert and there really is no need for four of us for this job. Once we have him, Stan will go to work on him and there will be enough help with the Doc. I'll ring you when we have what we need."

"That's okay then," Phil said, as he got the Google image of Croke Park back up on the laptop and went over the stadium again and again.

CHAPTER 21

Tom entered the lobby of the plush hotel where he was to meet David. He ordered a pot of tea and some toast and picked up one of the free newspapers that were scattered around on the tables. All the pages covered the airport bombings, with only small articles inside covering the house shooting and explosive find. *'David's done well to suppress the media coverage after the initial headlines,'* Tom thought as he read on. He was lost in his reading when David sat down in front of him.

"You startled me there for a second," Tom said.

"Jesus Tom! That Jack Maguire is some boy. I'm half glad that I wasn't around back in the day. You should have seen the state of the house when we got there; it looked like they were shot first with a sawn off shotgun using large shot cartridges and finished off with one to the head. It really is a pity that one of them got away and caused the carnage at the airport. We restrained two Special Branch members who were at the scene when our lads got there but it seems that an American who was with them slipped away during the commotion. They broke down during questioning after one hour and told us that they were acting under instruction from Assistant Commissioner O'Sullivan. They have given us long and detailed statements, after doing a deal on their future which will see them carrying out traffic duties in the furthest region of the country."

David recounted then how O'Sullivan had gone berserk when he got word of the arrest of the two Special Branch men by the armed response Units in Phibsboro.

O'Sullivan had stormed out of his office and he ran down the stairs, ignoring the lifts in his temper and pushed his way past the uniformed Garda on duty at the holding area of Garda Headquarters. He spotted David, the Commissioners Aide in the corridor.

"Here you," he shouted, "who the fuck do you think you are at arresting my men?"

David turned and looked at O'Sullivan: the veins were practically bursting in his neck, he noticed.

"Your men, Assistant Commissioner, your men you say?" David spoke in a calm voice, "two members of Garda **Síochána** have been arrested for questioning and if you have a problem with that, I suggest that you take it up with the Commissioner himself. He's in his office on the top floor of the building right now. You do know where that is, don't you?"

O'Sullivan stuck his face into David's, but seeing no fear or sign of backing down there, he turned on his heels and stormed away.

"You haven't heard the last of this," he roared, as he walked away. He could hear the applause and the jeers from both the uniformed and Armed Response men who had all been watching the encounter.

David observed O'Sullivan gather himself as he walked his way slowly back up the stairs. David knew his mind was racing, thinking out the situation that he now found himself in. As David left the building, he could see O'Sullivan looking out of the window, sneering at him.

After he'd finished recounting the story, Tom told him: "That's great news, David, but Jack Maguire is of the opinion that Croke Park is the target tomorrow."

And Tom went on to tell the whole story, as he had got it from Maguire.

"I've told him about the pending visit from the British Prime Minister, but he is absolutely convinced that it is Croke Park," he said.

"Jaysus! Tom, I can't see him been right. It has to be the British Prime Minister... unless he is acting the maggot and leading us astray."

"What for?"

"With intention being that it is him that is the real target, if you see what I mean, in his mind, the crimes of the past not been forgiven," David said.

Tom mused this over: could Jack Maguire be plotting to kill the British prime minister? He shook his head, "I don't think so, David, but what do I know?" he shrugged.

"I'll fill the Commissioner in on all this, Tom, and I will phone you straight away. Are you staying around town for a bit?" David asked.

"I'll hang around for a couple of hours," Tom answered, as David got up and left the hotel. A waitress approached Tom and he ordered a lunch and another pot of tea. It was only after he put his glasses on to finish reading the paper that he noticed the prices of the lunch on the menu.

"Oh my God!" he muttered to himself, "that's nearly a full day's wages."

But before he could cancel his order, the pot of tea with a fine china cup and saucer was placed in front of him.

"Lunch will follow shortly, Sir," the waitress informed him.

As he got back to reading his paper, Tom thought that this was going to be the most expensive free paper ever!

*

David sat with the Commissioner in his office on the top floor of Garda Headquarters. He had relayed to him the full discussion that he had with Tom Duffy. The Commissioner was sitting behind his desk, chewing on a pencil. He said nothing for several minutes as he digested all the information. David knew to stay quiet when his boss was chewing on a pencil because it meant that he was in deep thought.

"If Tom Duffy believes that Maguire is on the level and that he is not trying to pull a fast one regarding our visitor to Baldonnel, then that's the way we will go," the Commissioner eventually said. "But David, lets treble the amount of your emergency response teams around Baldonnel, particularly up on the high roads above Rathcoole that look down on the runway. Make sure that they can be seen constantly moving around that area and up the uniformed Garda presence on the roads leading in to the airport just to ensure that there are no surprises on the day."

"Leave that with me, Sir," David said, as he rose from his seat and left the office. He looked back as he walked out the door and he saw the Commissioner chewing like mad on the pencil. *'Clever man,'* thought David, *'he's leaving nothing to chance.'*

*

Jack asked Phil to get the Mosque in Phisboro up on the laptop and within seconds there it was; they scanned all around it, from the street at the front to the back, including the single storey building, which was the Mullah's house. They could see that it was surrounded by a five-metre-high wall and, as they both studied the picture in front of them, they could see that there was no way out the back, just an entrance in from the street and back out the same way. Jack pointed out what appeared to be a blind spot at the very back of the Mosque, the Mullahs house could not be seen from the entrance from the street, just as the Doctor had pointed out.

"That means that we will have cover if we have to take him with us," Jack mused.

"Look here," Phil said, pointing out a large white van parked up the road from the Mosque on the screen, "have you seen that van before?"

"It looks like the one that I recalled was parked on the street up from the house the other day," Jack answered.

"That's right," Phil said, "and if it didn't move when we were there that day, it more than likely will not move while we are with the Mullah. They are on observation duty only. Look here at the date in the corner; these images where posted up yesterday for the screen," Phil added.

The afternoon turned to evening and Jack saw Phil off to meet with Albert Green at the Croke Park Hotel.

"Happy hunting, Jack," Phil said, as he left.

Phil arrived at the Hotel just before nine o'clock. He spotted Albert sitting alone at the bar with the remains of a pint in front of him.

"Phil," Albert said, "it's great to see you. It's been a long time," he added nervously.

"Indeed it has," Phil replied, "let's sit down over here out of the way."

"Will you have a drink?" Albert asked.

"A 7 Up with ice will be fine, thanks," Phil answered.

When they were seated, Phil dismantled his mobile phone and began to fill Albert in on what was going on. As he relayed the story, he could see a look of complete disbelief come over Albert's face.

"Are you having me on?" Albert asked, shocked. "I think that this could just be a ploy to make my security company look bad and enable Jack Maguire's company to move in."

"Shut the fuck up with that nonsense, Albert, and listen intently to what I am telling you, or maybe you would like to tell Jack himself what your thoughts are?" Phil fumed.

"No, no, Phil," Albert stuttered, "I just can't take in what you are telling me."

"Well, take it in real quick," Phil said. "This is the final shot by the team of madmen who've been blowing up the city. We are working with the Garda on this – and you are now in the front line to help stop these madmen. So, just do as you are instructed and we will answer any questions after the match tomorrow."

Albert looked down at the floor. He knew that back during 'the war', if either Phil or Jack said something had to be done, then that was it, it had to be done with no question asked and he knew that what they said always worked out.

"Ok Phil, what do you want me to do?" he asked.

"Firstly, you have to make sure that every bag, no matter how small, is searched by your men, and have your phone with you at all times. I'll ring you first thing in the morning as things progress," Phil instructed.

Albert nodded his head.

"We have an outer ring of security where the first search can take place and another as you enter the

170

ground, where we can do a double search," he said, rising to what had to be done.

"Good man, Albert, now you are thinking. I'll see you in the morning when we'll know more on the situation," Phil said, as he left Albert sitting there in a state of shock.

Jack met up with the Doctor in the car park where he had left the van. The Doctor was dressed in his robes for prayer and had a bundle of similar clothing under his arm for Jack.

"These should fit you, Jack," he said, as he climbed into the van and handed Jack a pair of latex gloves.

"Good man, Doc," Jack said with a smile, "now you are learning this game."

Jack put the gloves on and then the clothes over his own and got into the driver's side of the van. Daylight was gone as they drove up the Old Cabra Road. Jack could see the stream of worshippers making their way home from the mosque. They picked up Stan who was waiting at a prearranged spot.

"There is no sign of Phil," Stan said, putting on his own gloves.

"He had to go and meet the guy who is in charge of the security at Croke Park," Jack informed them.

They parked the van just around the corner from the mosque and both Jack and the Doctor left Stan there. Jack had the stun gun in his hand, hidden in the pocket of the robe. He also had a circular hat on the top of his head, like others in the street. They walked towards the gates of the mosque and Jack noticed the white van parked further down the street. The last of the worshippers were leaving as Jack and the Doctor walked around to the single storey building at the back of the mosque. It was exactly 10.30 as they stood at the door.

"Are you ready, Jack?" the Doctor asked, nervously.

Jack took the stun gun out of his pocket and held it ready in his hand, hanging loosely by his side.

"Ready," Jack said.

The Doctor rang the doorbell and within a few seconds the door opened slowly and Jack looked at the man responsible for the suicide bombs. He had a fixed smile on his sharp-featured, tanned face.

"Ah, my brothers, welcome, do please come in," he said, standing to the side. His back was slightly turned from Jack as the Doctor walked in and Jack jabbed him with the stun gun in the side of the neck and pressed the button three times; the last time for his own satisfaction. The Mullah hit the floor, shaking as if he was having a fit. As this happened, the Doctor shut the door behind them. They dragged the then unconscious Mullah into what appeared to be the kitchen, sat him on a chair and tied him up with plastic electric cable ties that Jack had brought along for that purpose. He found a dishcloth and ran it under a running tap of water and when it was soaking wet, he tied it around the Mullah's mouth.

They did a quick check of the house: it was empty. Jack then called Stan in; he drove the van quickly into the grounds and stopped right outside the door of the house, hidden from the street.

The guys outside in the white van had mentally switched off as the last of the worshippers left and for that minute or so, they failed to see the green van drive through the gates.

"Now," Stan said, facing Jack and the Doctor, "this is my expertise." Pausing, Stan looked down at the tied up Mullah, he asked rhetorically, "I hope that either of you have no qualms about any of the methods that I may have to use this night to get the information that we need?"

"Stan, you work away and do whatever is required. We have until daybreak to work on this madman," Jack said and he turned on a small tape recorder.

"Carry on," the Doctor agreed.

Over the next few hours, Jack could not believe what he was seeing: Stan had most certainly done this type of work before. The wet towel smothered the screams. Time dragged on as the Mullah passed out from the pain on several occasions. Stan kept wetting the towel over the Mullah's head, causing him to believe that he was drowning. He had brought a small pair of pliers with him and proceeded to snap off the two small fingers on the Mullah's hands. The Doctor looked away as the blood spurted across the room and half a finger fell to the floor. Then Stan gripped the fingernail on the Mullah's thumb of his right hand and ripped it off. He continued with the nails on four more fingers before stopping to let the Mullah feel the pain. It was nine o'clock the next morning when the Mullah – after passing in and out of consciousness all night – finally broke. He confirmed that Croke Park was the final target and he also told them that he had been working hand-in-hand with an

American agent who had been filling his bank account with dollars and that he believed there was an Irish top level Government man involved. Jack had it all on tape. The Doctor looked at him in disgust.

"You led those young men into becoming suicide bombers, thinking that they were serving Allah and all the time you were accepting American dollars!" he shouted in outrage.

"Right, we need to move," Jack ordered. He opened the door of the house and walked out to the van. Stan climbed into the van and Jack and the Doctor roughly threw the Mullah in after him.

Jack drove out the gate, going the opposite way from the white van. He turned on the little blue box and, after a short distance, the all clear light came on. Jack then rang Phil and told him of the latest news.

"I'm with Albert at Croke Park as we speak," Phil told him.

"Good, keep your phone close to you and I'll keep you up to date as we move," Jack said.

"Croke Park!" Jack thought. As he speeded through the city, Jack reflected on how Croke Park stands as an iconic symbol of Irish National games, football and hurling and all games Gaelic and Irish. One section known as Hill 16 was built on the rubble of the GPO, which was the central point of the Easter rising in 1916. The stadium stands one kilometre from the city centre and Jack had grown up in its shadow in the north inner city. The history of the Irish Nation oozes from every brick he knew and the massacre of football supporters in what will always be known as Bloody Sunday by the forces of the British Government still lives in the memory of the Irish people. The stadium has grown in stature and size over the years until today where it now stands with a capacity of 82,300 people and is a three tier stadium with seven levels with over 2,000 tonnes of steel in the roof.

The amount of people that could be killed in an explosion, along with those that would be killed in the stampede to get out with the roof collapsing, would be incalculable. For a terrorist group wanting to send a sick message to the world, Croke Park on All-Ireland Day would be hard to beat.

Jack could now see why it could become a target for someone wanting to make that sick statement.

He then rang Tom Duffy.

"Tom, I was right," he said. "We lifted that man I spoke of and after many hours of talking to him with persuasion, he admitted that Croke Park is the target. He also told us that he is on the payroll of the Americans. We have it all on tape. You have to get moving Tom."

"I'm with you, Jack," Tom said, "I'll get back to you as quick as I can."

CHAPTER 22

As he digested the shocking news about the planned attack on Croke Park, Tom immediately rang David with the latest update.

"I didn't think that he would go that far, Tom. And I apologize for not getting back to you yesterday," David said. "I am getting in touch with the nearest Garda car to pick you up and get you here to headquarters... see you soon."

Within ten minutes, Tom was sitting in the back of the Garda car being driven at great speed with blue flashing lights through the countryside. In less than 20 minutes, he was walking into the Commissioner's office with David.

"Jesus! But that man can drive a car," he said of the Garda car driver with admiration. Just then his phone rang, he looked at the caller ID: it was Jack.

"Tom, I am leaving this madman tied up in a rubbish dumpster on level two of the James Hospital car park. It's outside door number ten, in his stocking on his right foot is the tape, the people with you will be very interested in what's on it. And Tom, you had better hurry up, he is unconscious at the moment and I don't know what time the rubbish truck collects the filth from these dumpsters."

Tom relayed to the Commissioner and David what Jack had just told him. David left the room straight away and instructed a Garda car on the street to proceed to and pick the tied up Mullah as quick as possible.

The Mullah woke to find himself upside down in a rubbish dumper. He could hear the sound of the van driving away. He momentarily smiled inwardly until he looked at his mutilated hand and the memory of the unbelievable pain that he had suffered returned. He thanked Allah when he discovered that his hands were tied to the front of him, this enabled him to tear the tape away from his mouth and then he was able to bite through the plastic cables ties that dug into his wrists. Suffering the pain of his chopped off fingers and ignoring the flow of blood, he pulled himself upright in the dumper and looked over the edge and saw in the distance a Garda car driving through the hospital car park with its lights flashing, as it moved towards him. He found that he could not pull the cable ties from around his ankles by hand, so he heaved himself up over the edge of the dumpster. As he let himself fall over the edge, he felt his stocking get stuck on a handle and fall off his foot back into the dumpster with the tape recorder in it. Looking at the car park, the Garda car was getting nearer to him and he had no time to retrieve the damning evidence, so he crawled away as far as he could and got under a car and hid.

177

The Mullah lay there – dressed in a pair of dirty boxer shorts, one stocking and a bleeding hand – trying to control his breathing. He could hear a man shouting that there was nobody there in the dumpster, but then another voice let out a shout that he could see a broken cable tie and a tape recorder.

"It looks like we're too late," a voice said.

"But there was someone here alright," the other said as he retrieved the tape recorder. "There's plenty of blood here."

"We better let them know at headquarters what's happened," the other voice added.

After he heard the car speed away, the Mullah crawled out from under the car and looked around him. He spotted an open door and hopped inside, as he sidled along the wall down the corridor, he tried to open several doors as he passed them. Then one finally opened for him, it appeared to be a locker room with a shower room in the corner. Pulling open some lockers, he found a pair of oversized trousers and a jacket along with a pair of shoes that were a size too small, but they gave him cover. He came upon a small towel, which again, using his teeth, he ripped in to strips and tied as tight as he could bear around his hand. He then used the edge of the metal lockers and scraped at the cable ties around his ankles until they broke. As he turned to exit the locker room, he noticed a wall mounted phone by the door. "Praise be to Allah," he said out loud to himself, as he lifted the receiver and tried the 0 button for an outside line. With great difficulty, he hit the buttons marking out his driver's mobile number and after several rings a voice answered.

"Hello?" the voice said tentatively.

"Caleed, this is your Amir calling... I have been kidnapped and mutilated by infidels who forced me to tell them of your mission... you must stay with it and see it through to the divine end... Do you understand me, Caleed? Allah is waiting to greet you..." the Mullah said.

There was a lingering silence.

"Caleed, talk to me?" the Mullah shouted as the phone went dead.

*

Caleed turned his phone off as the football match finished. He looked at it in his hand and thought of all the good times that he had in Dublin: drinking, doing lines of Coke and the lovely women. "Fuck this!" he said to himself, "I'm out of here."

He turned and began to run down the stairways.

*

As the Commissioner, Tom and David began to work out a plan, the Commissioner got a report from one of the state drivers dispatched to pick-up each Government Minister to take them to Croke Park, that his man was not going to the match.

"The little bastard!" yelled the Commissioner. "It's the Minister for Justice, Scully, who has been involved in this. He's not going to the match, which means that he will be last man standing if the bomb goes off, putting him in charge of the country if we don't stop this madness. Get my car, David... the three of us are going to Croke Park. Stay in touch with Maguire, Tom, it looks as if he has been right all along," he said.

The three men ran down the stairs to the car.

"As fast as you can to Croke Park," the Commissioner ordered the driver. "Stop for nothing or nobody."

He looked at his watch. "It's eleven o'clock… it's way too late to cancel the match," he said more to himself than to the others. "The gates for crew and supplies will long be opened and the minor teams will be in the stadium."

Without saying another word, they all knew the clock was fast ticking down to catastrophic mayhem.

*

Stan's friend in the ground staff – an ex-Croatian army office – had been watching all of the activity going on in the stadium. While he had been working from early morning rolling and marking the pitch, he had turned on the water sprinkler system and he looked around the empty stadium from the centre circle on the pitch: the only people moving around he could see were the media as they lay down miles of cable, the television cameras were being set up and tested; while the catering people were getting their stalls ready. The public address system was also being tested with Irish traditional music being played. He watched as the security people in each section carried out a more stringent search than usual, checking under all seats, stairways and lifts. He then noticed the Gardaí doing exactly the same again. *That seems odd,* he thought to himself. He now knew that Stan must be involved in something very serious and that was the reason for his request for assistance. He began to study the stadium in more detail and as a former soldier he worked out that the best time and place to cause maximum damage was the VIP area at the presentation of the cup. He looked up in that direction and could see some people setting up the podium and running microphone cables into it. He then made his way to the ground staff office to have a look at the schedule of workers and time of events for the day.

*

The Gardaí in the control room were amazed when the Commissioner walked in and took over control of the event. Instructions were given out to all Garda radios, by the Commissioner himself. He barked an order that every bag, big or small, was to be searched and that every man, woman and child were to be body searched as they came in. The Gardaí on duty snapped out of their attitude of a flippant match day to being on full alert. They knew that something was up if the Commissioner himself was issuing instructions and every one of them did not want to be the one to fuck up their position.

The Commissioner then called in all of the event controllers and the head of the security company to inform them that he was taking over full control of the day. The security head, Albert Green, then told him of the warning he had received and the measures that he had put in place. When queried by the Commissioner where his warning had come from, he replied that a man called Jack Maguire had been onto him and that, although he had found the warning hard to believe, he had acted on it.

"Good man, Mister Green," replied the Commissioner, "we are on the same road, so carry on with what you have in place and I will have Gardaí inside every turnstile doing a further check."

Albert could not believe what he was hearing: the Garda Commissioner, Jack Maguire and Phil all working in unison! *'This has to be extremely serious,'* he thought, which kicked him into extreme vigilant mode. He made his way to every spot of the arena, both inside and outside, where he had staff on duty and without telling them all that was happening, he then briefed them as to the importance of them carrying out their instructions to the letter.

CHAPTER 23

Jack contacted Phil.

"We're on our way to the ground," Jack said. "Can you meet us at Foster Avenue with some access all area passes?"

"Will do… I'll inform whoever is in charge of that barrier that your green van is to be waved on through, that way you will get into the stadium. All hell is breaking loose here, the Garda Commissioner himself has taken charge and there is definitely a feeling of nerves all round," Phil said.

"That's good, we should be there in five minutes," Jack said. As the van turned into Ballybough Road, a motorcycle Garda pulled in front of them and, with its lights flashing, sped them through the crowd which was building up as people left the pubs and walked towards the stadium. Jack looked at the crowd as he drove through them; there were families walking together, fathers, sons and young children decked out in their team colours. He could hear the nervous laughter and banter between the opposing supporters.

The familiar cry of "Hats, scarves or colours for sale," rang out along the route from the many merchandise sellers who sold there for generations. And, of course, the familiar cry of "Anyone buying or selling a ticket?" could be heard echoing throughout the streets as the ticket touts tried to earn a few euros. To Jack, these were all the sounds that were so familiar to his childhood of going to Croke Park for both Hurling and Football games. The fate of a lot of these people was now in his hands, he knew, and he had to believe that he had called this right.

A Garda Sergeant had the barriers at the entrance to Foster Avenue pulled back and the crowd stopped as the van sped through and into the stadium. A couple of supporters with a bit too much drink on board began banging on the side of the van, singing and asking for a lift into the stadium and also asking if there were any spare tickets inside.

Jack, Stan and the Doctor met up with Phil as they drove into the stadium. They put on their passes and entered the inner stadium. They split up: Jack and Stan went to meet his friend, the grounds man, and Phil and the Doctor began to make their way to the VIP area. The clock was ticking. It was half an hour to throw in and the ground was half full. The minor match was over, presentation done with no problems.

*

Tom Duffy was sitting in front of a bank of television monitors that covered every inch of the ground. He saw Jack and the other lads entering; he recognised Phil from the past and smiled to himself. He watched as they split up in the different directions. The Commissioner standing behind him had also seen the picture and asked Tom was he 100% sure that they were on the right side.

"I am," said Tom.

"I never thought we'd see the day that we would be working side-by-side with those guys to save the country," the Commissioner remarked.

"Let's hope that we can, Thomas," Tom replied. "Let's hope that we can."

Jack, Stan and his friend were in the staff office where they went over the list of contractors who had done work in the stadium, or who were working in the stadium that day. There were hundreds, so they looked at who had been working in the VIP area on the days leading up to and including the day itself. Stan then focused in on the exact presentation area, the speech podium itself. His friend remarked that he had seen a guy fixing what seemed to be a microphone to the podium earlier. The game was well under way and the noise of some 80,000 people meant that Jack could not hear Phil on the mobile phone. The three of them headed for the VIP area. Tom could see them walking at speed through the crowd but could not get them on the phone, he pointed them out to the Commissioner and told him what seemed to be going wrong, who looked and saw Jack throwing his mobile phone to the ground in a temper and shaking his head. The Commissioner spotted a Garda standing near Jack and he contacted him on the Garda radio to instruct him to go over to Jack and give his radio to him.

When the Garda approached Jack, he told him to "fuck off and mind his own business," but he was amazed when the Garda ignored the insult and handed him his radio.

"You have to tune into channel four," the Garda said.

On doing so, he recognised Tom's voice at the other end.

"The mobile phones are useless here," Tom said. "I have you on the screen in front of me and I can see your mate Phil and another guy making their way to the VIP area."

"Tom! Get the nearest Garda to Phil to do the same as you did with me, with the radios, so that way we will all have contact," Jack suggested.

Phil and the Doctor watched the ground fill up around them; the game had started and they could contact nobody, their phones were useless. A guy brushed passed the Doctor in a green boiler suit and the Doctor thought for a moment that he recognized him, but as he turned to tell Phil, the man disappeared.

"What's up?" Phil asked.

"Nothing, nothing, I just thought that I saw…" the Doctor's voice tailed off.

"Never mind nothing," Phil shouted. "What is it?" he demanded to know and they ran through the crowd in the direction that the Doctor last saw the man in the boiler suit going, but they could see nobody.

A Garda approached Phil and stopped him.

"We have access all area passes," Phil said, dismissively, "so what is the problem?"

"There is no problem. I have been told to give you this radio, you have to turn to channel four," the Garda said.

"Phil! This is Tom Duffy here. Jack cannot contact you as the phones are useless but I can relay any message," the voice on the radio said.

"Ok," Phil said. He then thought to himself, *'The infamous Tom Duffy!'*

"Tom! It's Jack here. My friend here beside me works in the stadium and he has told me that earlier he noticed a man fixing a microphone to the presentation podium and at that time, he was the only one in that area."

Tom listened to the message with the Commissioner, who replied that he could see nothing in that.

"Tom! For fuck's sake… when is the last time that you saw a cup presentation where the team captain was not handed a portable microphone? Tom, it's never a fixed mike on the podium," Jack shouted.

The Garda Commissioner jumped up from his seat.

"He's right on there, Tom. I captained my county many years ago and they hand you a mike to address the crowd. The podium has to be the place," he said excitedly. "We have to clear the VIPs," he then added, "Tom, the whole Cabinet will be wiped out if Maguire cannot find that bomb."

"If we start doing that now, we could start a panic and that could lead to a stampede of people trying to get out," Tom said, trying to calm down the rising hysteria.

The Commissioner looked at Tom.

"We could be fucked if we do and fucked if we don't, but we will have to make a call on it very soon," he said, and then turning to David, the Commissioner told him, "I know that you have some plain clothes boys on duty around the ministers... instruct them to be ready to grab whoever they are with, at a second's notice, and get them as far away from that area as quickly as they can. Instruct them to physically drag them out of there if they have to."

"I'm on it," David said, as he dashed from the room.

"Jaysus! Tom, if this goes wrong..." the Commissioner's voice trailed away.

"Cool head, Thomas, cool head. We can only do what we can do," Tom replied calmly.

The game was just over and the excitement of the crowd was at fever pitch. Jack and Stan were racing up a stairway against the flow of the losing team supporters exiting, when they passed a guy in a green boiler suit coming down, who was running faster than anyone else. On the next flight of stairs, they ran into Phil and the Doctor who told them about the green boiler suit guy. They turned and ran at speed back down the stairs. Phil relayed to Tom that all Garda nearby should stop the man in the green boiler suit at all cost. Jack and Stan then came upon a fight between two Gardaí and a guy in a green boiler suit. One of the Garda was bleeding heavily from the neck, having been stabbed, and the other was fighting off the attacker. Jack caught the boiler suit man with a kick in the jaw, sending him flying off the Garda. Stan jumped on him and held him down, but the boiler suit guy began fighting for his life – biting and thrashing all around him with his fists and feet, as he struggled free from Stan. As he stood up, Jack caught him with a savage kick in the balls that knocked the wind out of him.

This enabled both Jack and Stan to firmly grab him and hold him down. Unaware of what was going on, a group of supporters on their way out gathered around them, shouting to let the fella go. The group were getting close to helping the boiler suit man get free when Phil and the Doctor came on the scene. The Doctor immediately got to work to help the injured Garda, while Jack radioed in that they had got the guy and relayed the information that there were two Garda in a bad way and help was needed right away. Another Garda has come on the scene and wanted to arrest the guy.

"If he does that, Tom, with time flying on, we will not get the information that we need if we have to use conventional Garda methods," Jack said.

The Commissioner then grabbed the radio off Tom and spoke to Jack. Jack knew straight away who he was talking to. He told Jack that he was to make the call and do whatever he had to do to stop what was about to happen.

Tom looked at the Commissioner. "You do realise that they could kill this man or at the very least torture him?" he said

"Tom, we are the only two that heard what I said and I never gave any such instruction," replied the Commissioner.

The lads took the boiler suit man into a small room under the stairwell and instructed the Garda with them to stand outside the door and under no circumstances allow anyone in, no matter what he might see or hear.

"Now Stan!" Jack said. "I want you to persuade this guy to tell us where the detonation point is."

Before Stan could get started, they heard the final whistle go, meaning that there were only minutes left.

The Doctor said, "This is the Mullah's driver. If this guy wanted to do a suicide attack, then why did he not stay with the bomb?"

"You are right, Doc," Jack shouted, as he grabbed the boiler suit by the scruff of the neck. "I wondered where you had got to in all of this," Jack said as he dragged him out the door of the room and began to walk him back up the stairs the way he had come down. The boiler suit man began to struggle wildly and then all hands grabbed him and lifted him up and carried him back towards the VIP area. He began screaming in Arabic and the Doctor translated that he was crying for mercy and begging to be released, as they got nearer.

"Tell him that we will all die together unless he tells us where the bomb is," Jack shouted above the noise to the Doctor.

The crowd was on the pitch as the winning team battled their way through to walk up the steps to the podium.

As they carried boiler suit nearer the podium, his cries and screams increased. Tom, along with the Commissioner, were watching the monitors and could see the struggle on the stairway and the presenter of the cup awaiting the team, they then could see Jack pushing his way through the VIPs to the podium and knocking the Taoiseach aside, and then, just as the presenter was about to switch on the microphone and speak, Jack bent down beside the podium and picked up a hand mike from within and gave it to him. The presenter then welcomed the winning team. There was a huge sigh of relief in the observation room.

The stadium quickly emptied. Jack had tied boiler suit man's hands and feet together with electric cable ties and had him lying on the ground with his foot on his neck, the little bastard had cracked as they got near the presentation area and told Jack everything he needed to know. He told Stan, the Doctor and the grounds man to disappear into the departing crowd in case there was going to be any repercussion from their week's work. Phil stated that he would stay with him to see the end of this.

They were quickly surrounded by Gardaí, then the Commissioner, Tom and David walked through their ranks and they all snapped to attention. The Commissioner stood in front of Jack.

"Jack Maguire, I would like to shake your hand and thank you for all that you have done this week," he said, with his hand outstretched.

Jack looked at the outstretched hand for a couple of seconds. "Tom Murphy, you've done well for yourself," Jack said, shaking his hand.

The two of them smiled at each other. The Commissioner nodded his head and turned and walked away, followed by David.

The Garda then took boiler suit man into custody. That left Tom, Jack and Phil standing there.

"What will you do now lads?" asked Tom.

"Well, it's back to the Donegal hills for me, this city life is far too dangerous," said Phil with a smile.

"I have a little man and his mother to visit to try and get back on board with," Jack said.

"Well, good luck to the pair of you," Tom said, as he shook both men's hands. "I hope that we don't meet each other again," he laughed and he turned to walk away.

"One question, Tom," Jack said.

"What's that Jack?" asked Tom, turning back.

"Who won the match?"

"Well, we won this match, but I'm afraid the mad Mullah, as you called him, got away, but we got the tapes," Tom said.

Both Jack and Phil looked at each other and made their way to where they had left Mark Barry's van, got in and drove out of the stadium. Not a single word was spoken between the two men as they drove through the packed streets. Crowds of Dublin supporters filled the footpaths outside the pubs that lined the way from Croke Park to the city centre, pints of all the different drinks where raised in the air, there was singing and dancing all around, the atmosphere was electric. The two men parked the van in the ILAC centre car park, left the keys under the back left hand side wheel and walked out into the streets.

"What now mo chara?" Phil asked

"It's home for me, Phil," replied Jack, "tomorrow starts a new life for me."

"That's great to hear, bud," Phil said, "I'm going to leave you now, Jack. I'll get the late bus back to Donegal. Mark has my address, you can send my bag of stuff after me."

Jack looked at Phil, there was nothing more to be said. They gave each other a hug.

"Look after yourself, mo chara, you know where to get me," Phil said, as he turned and walked away through the crowds. Jack watched his friend walk away until he could see him no more. He turned and made his way towards his flat. Jack felt a really strong urge for a pint, all around him as he walked were people drinking in celebration of their team's victory. Unknown to all around, Jack could celebrate the greatest victory of the day – many of the people he passed would have been killed if he and his team had not won their battle, but to Jack his personal victory was that the vow that he had made to his young son as he lay in the hospital bed had been fulfilled.

"No!" Jack said to himself," there will be no drink for me," and he stepped out towards the flat.

CHAPTER 24

That evening, as Jack watched the news on the television, there was a news flash which caused him to sit upright on the edge of the sofa; the newsreader continued with a report of the arrest of the Minister for Justice. There was television coverage of a convoy of Garda cars led by a large Hummer type Garda vehicle smashing through a set of automatic metal gates and a Garda helicopter landing on the lush lawn fronting a mansion type house. The Garda Commissioner himself stepped out of the helicopter and walked briskly across the lawn to where a man in a black suit was exiting the mansion in a state of shock.

The camera then showed the Commissioner and a couple of other plain clothes Garda, one of whom Jack had seen alongside the Commissioner in Croke park that afternoon, put handcuffs on the disgraced Minster for Justice and lead him away towards a Garda car.

Jack smiled to himself. There would be hell to pay over the next few days, he knew. The Commissioner Thomas Murphy had wasted no time in beginning the sorting out of the nest of rats, he thought. He made himself a cup of tea and sat down to watch the highlights of the All-Ireland cup final.

At the exact same time that the Garda Commissioner was arresting Scully, five men in suits sat around a small table in a room in the depths of the American Embassy. The Ambassador and his Under Secretary sat opposite the Head of the C.I.A in Europe, the Garda Commissioner's friend sat to his right and another man who spoke not a word sat to his left.

The C.I.A Chief spoke in a low authoritative voice. "Thanks to the information we received from our good friends here in Ireland," he paused, looking to his right, "we are sending you both back to the State... here are your letters of resignation for you both to sign," he said, passing the two letters across the table, "and here is the use of my pen, which was given to me by the President himself for such occasions as this."

"Are you out of your mind?" the Ambassador spluttered, "I am the American Ambassador appointed by the President himself to Ireland. Who gave you the authority to even think of speaking to me in such a manner?" he said, slapping his hands angrily on the table.

The C.I.A Chief took a long slow deliberate breath. "You will do as you are told here, unless that is, you want to stand charges back home for abusing your position and have all your dirty secrets aired in a public Congress hearing, about your brother's involvement in the supply of planes to carry our troops to war and the creaming off of millions of dollars from that budget… no sir, I am not out of my mind, sign this document now," he ordered. He then looked at the Under Secretary, "And as for you, this gentleman on my left will escort you, this very minute, out of this building to a plane that we have waiting for you, to immediately take you back to the States. Now, depending on how helpful you are to my colleague's questions as you travel, will determine how you are treated when you touch down."

With that, the silent man stood up and walked around the table, he took the now former Under Secretary by the arm and stood him up.

"Mr Ambassador, you have to help me," he pleaded, as he was escorted out the door.

"The former Ambassador will be doing very well to help himself," he heard the C.I.A Chief say as the door closed behind him.

EPILOGUE

The airport was filled with the noise of thousands of travellers chatting and children's excited laughter, as they queued in a line to pass through security on their way to various holiday destinations. The clean cut, smartly dressed man with the shock of black curly hair and tanned complexion looked somewhat out of place amongst the holiday makers, as he bent down to pick up his briefcase from the baggage belt that passed through the x-ray machine.

"Excuse me, sir," a female voice called out.

His heart skipped a beat but he carried on walking, not looking back.

"Excuse me, sir," he heard again, but this time he felt a hand on his shoulder. He turned around slowly, filled with apprehension and looked into the face of a beautiful blonde girl in a security uniform. He noted from her name tag that her name was Christine.

"Yes, can I help you?" he asked, flashing a smile of snow white teeth.

"Your passport, sir, you left it on the security tray," she said, and handed it to him with a practiced smile. "I hope that you enjoyed your stay with us and that we see you again."

His breathing eased as he took the Saudi issue passport from her. "Not such a good one this time, but perhaps the next will be better," he said.

Flinching, he carefully turned away, protecting his gloved hand, as he remembered the excruciating pain of his missing fingers.

THE END

Printed in Great Britain
by Amazon